DAUGHTERS

(The heartbreak of human trafficking)

by

James W. Nelson

Dedicated to the mothers and daughters of the world

Biography

James W. Nelson was born in a farmhouse in eastern North Dakota in 1944. Some doctors made house calls back in those days. He remembers kerosene lamps, bathing in a large galvanized tub, and their phone number was a long ring followed by four short ones, and everybody else in the neighborhood could rubberneck. (Imagine that today!)

He was living in that same house on the land originally homesteaded by his great grandfather, when a savage tornado hit in 1955 and destroyed everything. They rebuilt and his family remained until the early nineteen-seventies when diversified farming began changing to industrial agribusiness. He spent four years in the US Navy, worked many jobs and finally has settled on a few acres exactly two and one half miles straight west of the original farmstead, ironically likely the very spot where the 1955 tornado first struck, which sometimes gives him a spooky feeling.

James has been telling stories most of his life. Some of his first memories happened during recess in a one-room country schoolhouse near Walcott, ND. His little friends, eyes wide, would gather round and listen to every hastily-imagined word. It was a beginning. Fascinated by the world beginning to open, he remembers listening to the teacher read to all twelve kids in the eight grades. Other than school papers, though, writing held off until the navy, where he kept a sparse journal. But the memory banks were beginning to fill.

About 1968 he interviewed his family and got their recollections of the 1955 tornado. His first piece and immediately rejected by Reader's Digest. But the vein had been opened. His first novel became a thousand-page behemoth, "hand-typed" four times. Then an electric—will wonders never cease?—typewriter, and two more drafts. The first computer arrived about 1980 (typewriter and monitor). One click and the story got typed automatically, but, still, *one page at a time*. The next three novels and about forty short stories came quickly.

INTRODUCTION

Thousands of young American girls have been abducted or lured from their normal lives and made into sex slaves. While many Americans have heard of human trafficking in other parts of the world -- Thailand, Cambodia, Latin America and eastern Europe, for example -- few people know it happens in the United States.

The FBI estimates that well over 100,000 children and young women are trafficked in America today. They range in age from 9 to 19, with the average age being 11.

UNICEF estimates that 2 million children per year are exploited in prostitution or pornography.

As many as 300,000 American youth may be at risk of commercial sexual exploitation at any time. Especially vulnerable are the homeless and runaways...one third of runaway youths—girls and boys both—will be lured into prostitution within 48 hours on the streets.

This novel is fiction. Any resemblance to any person or place is purely coincidental.

Debbie's story is particularly chilling. One evening Debbie said she got a call from a casual friend, Bianca, who asked to stop by Debbie's house. Wearing a pair of Sponge Bob pajamas, Debbie went outside to meet Bianca, who drove up in a Cadillac with two older men, Mark and Matthew. After a few minutes of visiting, Bianca said they were going to leave.

"So I went and I started to go give her a hug," Debbie told "Primetime." "And that's when she pushed me in the car."

As they sped away from her house, Debbie said that one of the men told Bianca to tie her up and said he threatened to shoot Bianca if she didn't comply.

"She tied up my hands first, and then she put the tape over my mouth. And she put tape over my eyes," Debbie said. "While she was putting tape on me, Matthew told me if I screamed or acted stupid, he'd shoot me. So I just stayed quiet."

Unbelievably, police say Debbie was kidnapped from her own driveway with her mother, Kersti, right inside. Back home with her other kids, Kersti had no idea Debbie wasn't there.

"I was in the house. I mean, it was a confusing night. I had all the kids coming in and out. The last I knew she had come back in," Kersti said. "It was just so weird that night. I mean, I normally check on all my kids, and that night I didn't. I should have."

Debbie said her captors drove her around the streets of Phoenix for hours. Exhausted and confused, she was finally taken to an apartment 25 miles from her home. She said one of her captors put a gun to her head.

"He goes, 'If I was to shoot you right now, where would you want to be shot -- in your head, in your back or in your chest?'" Debbie said. "And then I hear him start messing with his gun. And he counted to three and then he pulled the trigger. And then I was still alive. I opened my eyes, and I just saw him laughing."

Debbie said she was then drugged by her captors and other men were brought into the room, where she was gang raped.

"And then that's when I heard them say there was a middle-aged guy in the living room that wanted to take advantage of a 15-year-old girl," she said. "And then he goes, 'Bend her over. I want to see what I'm working with.' And that's when he started to rape me. And I see more guys, four other guys had come into the room. And they all had a turn."

Acording to ABC Primetime February 9, 2006

DAUGHTERS

(The heartbreak of human trafficking)

by

James W. Nelson

Emma was eighteen. Her birthday had just passed. Just another day. No party, no cake or candy, no balloons or gifts, but she did get one card from a person from deep in her past. But he was just a vague memory, and not somebody any longer important to her. Yet, on very rare occasions, something would happen to cause his face to flash through her mind, like a blink. But no more than a blink.

But not a lot of time to feel sorry for herself. According to Merle, her Aunt Evelyn's boyfriend, the back door of this house would be unlocked. It was. Carrying her mop in one hand and the pail with the cleaning stuff in the other, she entered.

And right away was hit with a smell that many of the houses she cleaned had. A bachelor smell. She didn't know what caused it. Not exactly an *unclean* smell, but a smell. She didn't like it, and she didn't especially like cleaning bachelors' houses. Not that she especially didn't like bachelors, she just rather would clean houses where children lived. She just felt more at ease where families resided. But she lived with Aunt Evelyn, and several of Merle's friends were bachelors. They needed their houses cleaned, and Emma needed the extra money. She worked for a cleaning company but wanted to enter college in another year so she took the extra jobs too, and did what she had to do. She paid rent to Merle but mostly could save her money.

The other time she was at this house she had gotten the cleaning done and got out before the owner came home, and she was glad, for as she was walking away she had met a man driving an older blue and white pickup. The man had stared at her, just gaped, and kind of scared her, but at least he hadn't stopped. So she wanted to get done cleaning and get out again. But the house was a mess, everywhere. So three hours later she still had the living room to clean and it was getting close to five. The man, before, had come home a little after five.

At five-thirty she finished, packed her cleaning stuff in the pail and headed for the door. Through the window she saw the blue and white pickup enter the driveway, just barely. Then the man jumped out immediately and came to the door so fast...

"Well, hi there, sweetie." The man was tall, at least six feet, had black hair, and needed a shave, and was smiling, but it wasn't a warm smile, more like a smile of triumph.

There would be no getting past him. Had she thought she would have gone out the front door, but she didn't think, and she —*yet*—had no reason for apprehension, so why did she feel apprehensive? So she answered, "Hi...." Her mind flew deep into her past to that memory growing more vague every day, to when she still had her mom, and her mom's boyfriend, to the memory that she always felt safe with Mom's boyfriend, and, especially, loved and cared about. His face flashed by, like a blink, never longer.

"Well," Emma gripped her mop and pail, "I have to get home...." She stepped to his left, if she could just...

But he stepped in front of her, "Merle tells me you just had a birthday."

"Yes." Emma's hands tightened.

"Merle said you just turned eighteen." His smile changed, to not a smile at all.

"Yes." Emma made plans. If she threw the pail at him then she could hit him with the mop. She'd lose all her cleaning stuff, but, "I need to get home, sir."

"Hey, sweetie, you don't have to call me '*sir*'. My name's Jackson." His eyes had lost all smile, just a cold stare now, "I'd like you to stay awhile. Hell, I'd even sing '*Happy Birthday*' to you, baby. A girl only reaches eighteen once, you know."

"Sir, I want to go home." No longer was there any doubt in Emma's mind that she would have to fight her way out. Her body stiffened. With her left hand she threw the pail at Jackson's face, screamed, then grabbed her mop with both hands and hit him in the face, and screamed again. And she heard her own scream. It reminded her of the screams made by professional female tennis players when they slammed that ball back at their opponents. She had always planned to maybe play professional tennis someday, and she *had* played, a little, in high school, and had planned to play even more in college, and had planned to practice that scream, but never had, until that moment hitting Jackson with the pail and kind of a little scream, and then the mop with a bigger really *good* scream.

Jackson wasn't expecting such an animal sound either, and fell back from the scream more so than from the pail and mop, "Little bitch!"

Emma moved immediately and, almost, made it. She even got the door open and pushed it, but only a little before Jackson's hand clamped onto her left wrist. She screamed a third time as he jerked her back into the kitchen and pulled the door closed again.

"Stop that screaming!" Jackson swung an open-handed slap.

Emma screamed again but this time it wasn't a professional tennis player's scream, but just a frightened little girl's scream. For just a second that deep memory came back. She saw her mom's boyfriend's face again. Just that flash! She wished he would help her. But he couldn't. He probably didn't even remember her—but he did! He sent cards! He was a kind, loving, man, not like this guy! When she fell back her hand landed on a bottle that she somehow hadn't noticed when she cleaned the kitchen. She gripped it by the neck and held it ready to throw as she moved again toward the door. If she could just get close to the door she could throw it and then run.

She reached the door. Jackson stood about six feet away. His eyes were staring but very calm. Emma felt he should have been showing a little tension, but he wasn't. He was just... waiting. She threw the bottle, screamed her professional tennis player's scream and turned the door knob—locked! When had he locked it? It wasn't locked a minute ago!

The bottle missed Jackson. He took one step and swung open-handed again and struck the left side of her face, then came back and struck the right side of her face, "Damn little bitch!"

No more *good* screams left her. Now, again, just frightened little girl sounds. Jackson grabbed her right arm and spun her around, and started pushing her toward the bedroom. At the door he pushed her hard, so hard she flew across the room. Her legs hit the bed and she fell onto it. She rolled onto her right side, drew her legs and body into a fetal position. She felt blood in her mouth. She knew there wasn't a lot of fight left in her. That deep memory flashed back to her yet again. Her mom's boyfriend was a kind and good, man, but if all he ever wanted to do was send her birthday cards he must not really care about her...he must not *love* her!

Jackson stood just inside the bedroom door, staring at her, "There's no way out of this room, little girl, so, if I was you I would just lay there quietly. I have to make a phone call, and then

I'll be back, and I'll have a present for you, and you, little girl, are going to give a present to me. It's *my* birthday today." He pointed at her, "So just be good and lay still. I haven't hurt you yet, but if you try to hurt me again, then I will hurt you." He left the room but didn't close the door.

One window but likely it didn't open. Had she thought she would have tried it when she cleaned the room, but she didn't think, and why would she have? She couldn't go around planning escapes from every house she cleaned. But, she guessed, she should have with this one. Jackson's voice came from the other room. Why was he making a call now? Then she heard one word *"Fletcher"*. She should try to remember that name, and at least *try* the window.

Too late. Jackson appeared in the doorway again, "Yeah, she's a little babe all right. Cherry red hair and lots of it. Your customers will love her—" *Customers?* "Yeah, oh about five feet, five inches, weighs about a hundred-ten maybe twenty, blue eyes, buxom, for her youth. Just the size and shape your customers will love."

Why was that man describing her? Emma was frightened earlier, but now she was beginning to feel real fear, and began looking around for another weapon—

Jackson stomped to the bed, "Don't be looking around for escape, little baby, cause you ain't going nowhere!" Then into the phone, "So when ya gonna get here?"

Who was coming? And why? An ache began in Emma's stomach. She had been pretty sure she was going to get hurt, but also had assumed he would then let her go, but now…now she didn't know anything.

"An hour?" Jackson said into the phone, "Great! That gives me plenty of time to get this little vixen broke in good, and you have your cash ready when you get here!" Jackson shut the phone off, then walked to the dresser to lay it down.

Emma was off the bed in a blink and heading for the door. Jackson got there first, and this time he hit her hard with a closed fist. Emma saw stars and hit the floor.

****

When Emma awoke she had no idea of anything. She was in a moving vehicle. She could feel that. Her hands were tied behind her. She couldn't really move at all. Her head hurt, and she hurt between her legs, and was wet down there. And she was cold. She managed to look down. In the dim light the wetness looked dark, like blood. Right, the good man Jackson had taken her virginity. At least she had not been really awake to experience it. At least she had not had to see his face, and she would never forget that face, and she hoped someday she would have the chance to kill him. And she would, with no remorse.

She tried to move and realized her feet were tied too, and tied *to* her hands. At least they—whoever they were—had given her a mattress to lay on. Not exactly a clean one though, and it smelled of…she didn't know what. She was able to wriggle though, and moved enough to be able to see forward, and determined she was in a van with no side windows. In the seats in front she saw a woman passenger, and not tied up, like herself.

The woman looked back, "Our new little angel has awoken, Fletcher."

Fletcher, the same name Emma had heard Jackson say. A woman maybe would be willing to help her, "I have to go to the bathroom," Emma said.

"You'll get your chance, sweetums, but just hold it for now. I know you can."

The man glanced back, "There's a rest area in about twenty miles."

Emma saw his eyes. Apathetic eyes. She felt pretty sure the man would not care about her plight at all. She hoped the woman would, "I can't hold it that long."

The woman looked back again, "Then just go ahead and pee your pants, sweetums."

The bitch! So that's what the smell was. Urine. Other girls

had lain here just the same as her, and had peed their pants. Who *are* these cruel people? But Emma wasn't about to pee her pants. She did have to but was pretty sure she could wait twenty miles.

Sleep came, and dreams. She was walking and skipping between her mom and her mom's boyfriend. She was so happy. Often they would stop walking and all hug at the same time. How she had loved those hugs, to be hugged by her mom and her mom's boyfriend at the same time. How happy her mom had become after that good boyfriend walked into their lives, and how happy Emma became too…but then Mom died.

Then the dream changed. Her mom lay in a casket, and Emma was standing by the casket between Aunt Evelyn and her mom's boyfriend, and Mom was just lying in the casket and not moving. Mom had gone to Heaven Aunt Evelyn said, and she wasn't coming back. Why, Emma wondered. She was so young then and she didn't really even understand about Heaven.

Then it was just her and Mom's boyfriend walking, but he always held onto her hand, and still hugged her a lot, and let her hug him, and he took her places…and then Aunt Evelyn came and took Emma's other hand, and stopped them. Good, then she can walk and skip between Aunt Evelyn and Mom's boyfriend, and maybe Mom's boyfriend will become Aunt Evelyn's boyfriend and they can all live happily ever after.

But they didn't even start walking. Aunt Evelyn held onto Emma's left hand and reached over and pulled her right hand from her mom's boyfriend's hand, and then Mom's boyfriend just disappeared.

Emma's dream stopped because she suddenly had to pee, really bad, "I have to pee!" she cried, "Right now! Please stop! Please!"

The woman turned around, "Just let it go, sweetums."

You bitch! You awful bitch! But Emma absolutely could not hold it, and had to let it go, and *felt* it going, felt every last drop going. It made her wetter, and it made her mad, and then it cooled and made her colder. Then she didn't want to but started to cry.

"Better cry now, baby," the woman said, "Because where you're going there won't be many chances to cry."

Then, to add insult to injury, the man also turned back, "And we passed that rest area a long time ago, but you were sleeping so good we didn't have the heart to wake you." Then he laughed.

Someday my mom's boyfriend will kill both of you! Emma surprised even herself at that thought, that she could even imagine, even subconsciously, that her mom's boyfriend would ever come for her, and save her, and again, if all he cared to do was send her birthday cards then he must not care very much! He must *not* love her at all!

The smell of her own urine reached her. She choked, and began to cry again, but silently. She didn't want those two cruel people to hear her. Sleep came again, and the same exact dream came again.

****

The van slowing down and turning woke Emma. She had dreamed and dreamed and dreamed, and always the same dream, with her Aunt Evelyn pulling her away from her mom's boyfriend's hand, which always caused him to disappear. She knew there were happier memories, many of them. But this dream was strong, even though—except for the hugging—it wasn't a true memory. But the dream she felt ensured her that Mom's boyfriend would never come for her. A little part of her mind kept saying he would, but that other little part kept saying he would not, because *why* would he? He didn't know her, he didn't remember her, and he thought all that was necessary was to send birthday cards!

The van stopped but kept running. The man left. Emma could see brighter lights but she didn't want to rise up. She didn't want to give the woman cause to speak again.

After about five minutes the man returned. They drove a short distance and stopped again. Then the engine stopped. So they were somewhere, maybe just for the night.

Emma didn't move and kept her eyes closed tight. She could sense at least one of them coming to the back of the van, then the voice of the woman, "OK, sweetums, we're at a motel for the night. I'm going to untie you but don't try anything funny because Fletcher is here too. We're going to bring you into the motel, clean you up and give you some dry clothes—"

"The clothes will come later," Fletcher interrupted.

"Oh, yes, right," the woman said, "First we're going to have a little training session."

Training?

"And *then* we'll give you clean clothes."

Emma, of course, did not know what they meant. Way in the back of her mind she was beginning to comprehend her future, but she refused to allow such thoughts to enter her conscious mind. She kept trying to think of *happier* things, happy and fulfilling things she had planned for her own future. But happy thoughts would not long stay with her, and after those short-lived happy thoughts were gone again she was left with the wondering of how many young girls had been forced to lie on this same smelly, urine-soaked mattress, now with the smell of her own urine added.

The rope left her ankles. She moaned. Her first wish was to straighten out her legs.

"Just hang on there, sweetums. You'll get your chance to move around, a little."

Emma tried to cooperate as fully as possible, but also was planning to try to escape too. Maybe she could get out the back door of the van. But her legs felt half numb. She probably would fall down, and get punished. She felt these people would not hesitate to punish her, maybe even kill her.

The rope left her hands. She heard a click. It sounded like a sound from the television, like that of a hammer being pulled back on a gun. She opened her eyes.

"Yes, sweetums," the woman said, "This is a gun, with a silencer." She held the gun sideways and exhibited the extra long barrel, "And I will not hesitate to shoot you." She pointed toward the front, "Fletcher is waiting for you by the driver-side door, so just go quietly up there and he will escort you into the room."

Emma did as she was told, but would continue to weigh every possibility of escape. But nothing. The instant her feet touched the parking lot surface Fletcher slapped handcuffs on her left wrist and had the other half on his right wrist, and held the chain in his right fist. She was helpless but to walk to the door of the motel room.

Inside was dingy. Not exactly unclean she didn't think, but if *she* worked for the motel the room would not look even dingy. Then, given her situation, she felt really strange for having such a thought, about cleaning, but cleaning was what she did to earn money.

The woman soon joined them and locked the motel door, "OK, sweetums, we're going to take the cuffs off and you are going to get in the shower, and you're going to wash yourself inside and out." She hesitated, then touched Emma's shoulder, "Inside and out. Do you understand me?"

"Yes." Emma didn't know why she was emphasizing. She knew how to wash herself.

"I don't think she understands, Fletcher. Get the cuffs off. I'll go in there with her."

Fletcher removed the handcuffs. The woman pointed to the bathroom door. Emma went to it and entered. The first thing she saw was the window. It wasn't an opening kind but she felt she maybe could have gotten through, but maybe would have gotten cut too. It seemed these two knew how to handle prisoners.

The woman came in right behind her and held out a plastic bag, "Put your clothes in here, everything, including your shoes."

Emma did as she was told. She took all her clothes off, then stood with her right hand and arm covering her breasts and her left as much as she could of her front, and waiting to be told what to do next.

"What about the necklace?"

Emma had forgotten the necklace. She had worn it forever, and never took it off except to go in the shower, but she had forgotten the situation she was in and felt horrified of losing it, "It, it…was a gift…."

"Take it off!"

"Please…!"

"The woman snatched it and jerked it free, breaking the chain, glanced at it then would have thrown it into the bag.

"No! Please! It was a gift from my mom…!"

The woman looked at it again, then enclosed it in her hand, "All right. I'll keep it for you." She nodded toward Emma's body, "You might as well stop trying to cover yourself, sweetums, because people are going to want to gaze upon that yummy body of yours."

Emma felt a pressure streak to her head, and felt her face redden and her stomach tighten. The woman had just told her, bluntly, what her future held, but Emma continued to block it from her conscious mind.

The woman then turned to the man, "Fletcher, get rid of these. They stink!"

So she wasn't getting her clothes back. She guessed it didn't matter.

"Now drop the modesty act, sweetums." The woman pointed, "And get in the shower."

Emma did as told, but began to wonder what had happened in this woman's life to cause her to be so…she didn't know, so cold, and cruel. She appeared to have no feelings at all, no emotions, maybe was born that way, maybe was a sociopath. She had read about them in her psychology class, one of her favorite subjects. Psychology and tennis. Those were her goals, and still remained as goals. But she felt them slipping away and going into another garbage bag, like the one that held her soiled clothes. She would never see those clothes again, but the bag with her goals…she would not give up on them, not yet.

Once in the tub she turned to close the curtain. The woman, with no feelings, no remorse, nothing, stopped her, "Just partway, sweetums. I'm going to watch you."

"That's not my name!" Emma snapped before she thought, but she was sick of that cruel woman calling her such a cutesy name, as if they were best friends.

The woman slapped her, from both directions, then again. On the third slap Emma slipped and fell, and hit her elbow on the tub enamel. "You can forget your real name, sweetums. In your future line of work you'll have another name. We haven't decided what yet."

"Do I get a vote?"

The woman laughed, "Stand up and get to washing."

Again Emma did as told, and began soaping herself down, and used a wash cloth to scrub herself, then washed the soap off, and thought she was done, but got a back hand that brought blood.

"Soap down again, sweetums, and I told you to wash yourself inside and out—"

"I did!"

"I know you did, but you didn't go deep, so *do* it! Or I will do it for you…."

"All right." The second soaping Emma made a special attempt to do it right.

"That's better. Now get out of there and dry off." The woman pushed the shower curtain all the way open and stepped back.

Again Emma tried to cover herself.

Again the woman laughed, and shook her head.

Emma was beginning to hate her. She finished toweling

off, covered herself, and waited, "Do I get some clothes?"

The woman stepped back and pointed, "Get on the bed."

Emma walked across the floor, reached the bed and sat down, and received another slap, then a push, and that quickly both her hands were grabbed and handcuffs were slapped on both her wrists, Fletcher on the other side of the bed attached her right hand to that bed post, and the woman attached her left hand to the other bed post. She no longer could cover her nakedness. The thought horrified her. Then handcuffs were also attached to her ankles, and attached to the lower bedposts, which spread her legs. She closed her eyes…*this can't be happening.*

But it was.

"Now, sweetums, there'll be no more modesty. There's no time for it, and by the time Fletcher gets through, you'll be willing to walk right down the street naked. And, if that isn't enough then I'm here to finish the job."

Emma heard a slap. She opened her eyes. The woman again slapped her open palm with what looked like an adult toy, something she had once seen in one of her Aunt Evelyn's boyfriend's catalogs. Merle, that asshole! She had never *liked* him! Just seeing the adult toy, a latex penis, she now saw, made her stomach tighten even more.

"Of course," the woman went on, "Even if what Fletcher does to you *does* quiet you down, I'm still going to finish the job." She slapped her open palm again, then turned and looked at the man.

Now down to his shorts, he held a real penis in his hand.

To Emma, the dark, slimy-looking thing he held was not real, and what the woman held was not real. Emma felt her mind slipping. Maybe if she thought hard enough she could die, and stop this terrible thing from happening. She jammed her eyes shut tight. She at least didn't have to look at them. She felt the bed sag on the side where the man was. She knew he was coming, and that she would not be able to stop him, no matter how she wished for insanity to come and stop her life.

She felt the man moving over her right leg. She wanted to kick him! She wanted to kill him! She wanted to scream…she did! She screamed. Instantly the woman slapped her head with the latex penis "Be quiet, little sweetums. There are no cops in this town, and we have an arrangement with the motel manager. So you can scream all you want and nobody will help you. But, if you insist on screaming, each time you do I will hurt you worse, so just don't do it, and remember, I have the gun with the silencer. So, if you become too uncooperative, I will just kill you."

With the end of the woman's speech Emma felt something wet between her legs, then something probing inside her, then more wet, then she felt the man crawling over her, then entering her. She gritted her teeth, and held her eyes shut so tight she thought they would surely break. The man didn't take long to do his job. He must be a weenie. Emma felt like laughing, but as soon as he withdrew the woman took over with the fake one.

What was happening went on for two hours. First the man, then the woman, then the man, then the woman. Emma kept her eyes jammed shut through it all and said not another thing. Finally the man said, "That's enough."

When Emma opened her eyes she wasn't planning to speak. But it came out anyway. She looked at each of them, "My daddy will come to get me, and he will kill both of you awful people."

Both stared at her. "The only daddy you have is '*Merle*', that loser-buddy of Jackson's," the woman said, "And, also, according to Merle, through Jackson, your mommie died years ago." Then the woman stopped talking, but kept staring, as if expecting some sort of answer, then kind of laughed and looked away, "So nobody is coming for you, little sweetums, and the sooner you accept that the better off you'll be."

Emma, actually surprised at what she had said, wished she could think of something else to say, but with what she *did* say she had noticed their expressions change—if only for a second or two, as if they believed her. She wished *she* could believe it too….

****

Emma was left as she was on the bed till morning, then was given dry clothes but no shoes. The trip to wherever they were going took two more days tied and lying on that smelly mattress, and one more night at a motel, where the same so-called training session took place. Emma knew she had no choice, so took it as well as she could and cooperated. When they arrived at their destination she hoped the '*training*' would stop. It didn't. The ordeal went on for another day and two nights with different men. The same woman stayed, gave orders, and guided some other young girls to degrade her as well, and if the girls didn't do as told they were also punished. She remembered one older woman who did not exactly participate, more like just an observer, and once yelled at one of the men who she must have thought was being too abusive. But what did it matter she wondered? But part of her, she knew, still mattered, and she would remember that one woman. If she ever saw that one woman again she would ask for help. When Emma finally was taken to a lonely house in the country she had no idea even what part of the country she was in. But among other girls *like* her she at last felt somewhat safe, and was allowed to sleep until she awoke.

****

But it wasn't good, restful, sleep. Emma's dreams were of unhappy times. No, Merle never molested her. He also never loved her, and not that Emma wanted his love, but he *was* her main male presence and influence. And Merle never abused her Aunt Evelyn, not physically, but he also never said anything nice to her, and they never hugged or showed any affection for each other, not in Emma's presence, anyway, so her dream went to her mom and her mom's boyfriend, and the memory of the three of them hugging at the same time—then Aunt Evelyn appeared and her mom's boyfriend disappeared.

That dream ended and Merle appeared again. He was smiling, at least his face was different, and his words, "That guy wants you to clean his house again." That guy, that guy's name was Jackson, but Merle didn't say it. He just handed her the address on a piece of dirty paper. Then Emma's dream returned to that day. She remembered more. She remembered the face, the eyes, the eyes that held no emotions, no love, no nothing—

"Emma…?"

At last, someone calling her by her real name.

Emma's dream switched back, way back, she was small and anticipating the new Walt Disney movie, but she couldn't think of the name, but she was happy just thinking about it, knowing she would be happy for a little while watching it, but Aunt Evelyn said, "You can't go." *Why*? She wondered, but her aunt gave her no reason. Emma remembered being broken hearted, and remembered other times when she wasn't allowed to do something she really wanted to. Why? *Why? WHY?*

"Emma, wake up."

Emma knew she was dreaming. She heard the voice and knew it was gentle and friendly, but even in her dream state she knew what awaited her when she awoke, so she didn't *want* to wake up, and fought it.

"Emma, please wake up."

A girl's voice, young, like herself.

"Emma, you need to wake up, and eat something. You have to keep up your strength. They'll keep hurting you no matter what, but they'll hurt you worse if you don't cooperate—Emma!"

Someone shook her, but she did not want to awaken, "My daddy will come for me." She said that very low and had not meant to say it at all. She had no idea about her daddy, and knew she was thinking about her mom's boyfriend, the man who never, ever, tried to see her, the one who thought sending birthday cards was enough—!

"Emma!"

Emma opened her eyes and saw an angel with generous blonde hair backlit by one bright window, "Who are you?" she asked, "Where am I?" The person sitting on the bed beside her looked so kind and innocent and trustworthy that Emma wanted to hug her, so she raised up and put her arms around that angel, and felt arms go around her and hold her tight.

"I'm Alexis, Emma, and I'm trapped here just like you, but I can be your friend…if you want."

Emma leaned back and looked again at that angelic face, "I want," then she leaned into the hug again and Alexis continued hugging her back.

"You mentioned your '*daddy*', Emma…but I hate to tell you, '*daddies*' never come here. Two of the girls here had abortions, and their '*daddies*' kicked them out. There's fourteen of us in three different houses, and no '*daddy*' has ever came."

Emma knew she was being unrealistic, and she knew her mom's boyfriend would never come. Yet she wondered why she had been so consistently dreaming about him, but she should probably try to totally block that memory, "Where are we, Alexis? Do you know?"

"We're in a house not too far from Las Vegas. Some of us go to town every night to sleep with men—and sometimes women—who pay for us—"

"You're prostitutes?"

"Not just *us*, Emma, but now you are too."

In the back of Emma's mind she had feared that but she had refused to even think about it. Now it seemed like she had no choice, and tightened her arms around Alexis.

"I know you feel safe right now, Emma, with me, but they separate us too—"

"Why?"

"To keep us from developing too close of a friendship."

"These people are so cruel."

"Yes, they are." Alexis tightened her hug, "But now you have to get up and eat some breakfast. Your first night here you were allowed to sleep and relax, but that's over now. They'll be back for you at 1 PM, and that's just two hours from now. You have time to eat, shower, take your birth-control pills, and get dressed."

A sob escaped Emma. She just couldn't help it, "Birth-control?"

Alexis tightened her hug even more for a few more seconds, then patted Emma's shoulder, "Yes, Emma, they don't want us to get pregnant. But don't worry. You and I can be friends. But remember, we can't show our friendship too much. If they notice they'll separate us right away, and even some of the other girls might tell on us. They think they get privileges for telling! But they don't." Alexis patted Emma's shoulder again then relaxed the hug and stood, "Here's a robe. You can eat breakfast in this. They bring us fast-food twice a day. I saved some for you. Oh, and shower shoes." She pointed to under the window, "Those haven't been worn, that I know of, and you definitely want to protect your feet here."

Emma sat up and swung her legs out, then realized she was naked and covered herself with the bed cloth.

"I know you'll try to keep yourself covered, Emma, and so do I, but sometimes it's hard." Alexis walked to the door, then turned, "They will allow us to share this room, Emma, as long as we don't appear too friendly. We can be friendly in here, but not out there." Alexis waved, "See you later…."

Emma returned the wave, "Thank you, Alexis," and watched her angelic new friend disappear. When the door closed she grabbed the robe and put it on, then walked to the window. The first thing she saw was mountains in the far distance, then noticed the sun, still to her left and it was still morning she thought, so she was facing south. She didn't know how knowing her directions could help her but she wanted to know. The only other thing outside was another building that didn't look like a house. Alexis had said there were three houses, but she doubted that building was. While she stood there her feet found the shower shoes and slid them on.

"…*protect your feet here.*" What Alexis had said almost made it sound like *while* we're here, as if she knew they were eventually leaving, but she knew that wasn't what she meant. Emma pulled the robe closed and crossed her arms under her breasts and held herself, and released a breath that shook a little. Yes, she was still frightened, but not as much since she had met Alexis. She checked the window for stability, then pushed up, slightly. It moved. She felt it would move all the way and she knew she could break the screen. When the time came…well, the *time* wasn't yet. She would learn about this place, and learn about the other girls, and when the time *did* come she would take Alexis with her and they would escape.

****

Emma carefully stepped from the shower and wrapped a towel around her, not a very lavish one but at least it got her mostly dry. Then she wrapped herself in her robe again and stepped from the shower room. Several other young girls looked up. Nobody smiled, not even Alexis, but she knew why, so she didn't smile at anybody either, and almost made it to her room…

"So you finally got a roomie, huh, Alex, how *is* she?"

Emma looked back but couldn't pick out the speaker.

"We don't really know each other yet," Alexis answered.

"Ha! You must have spent a half hour in there; you certainly must have gotten a taste!"

Taste?

Emma didn't know what she meant by that but was able to pick out the speaker. A taller girl with long brunette hair, kind of a *mousey* look, and maybe a little too slim. The girl wasn't that pretty. Emma wondered what she was even doing there, then chided herself for wondering such a thing.

Alexis didn't answer back, so Emma entered their room. Next time they were together she would ask what the girl meant by *taste*, although she had a funny back-of-the-mind feeling of what it did mean. But, as she was doing quite often lately, she refused to think too much about it.

The closet didn't hold much selection of clothes, so she

returned to the door, opened it but didn't care to go back, so just called out, "Alexis, what clothes should I put on?"

Alexis glanced at a wall clock, then, "Heather will soon be here with your clothes, Emma. Don't worry."

"You better go in and comfort your little charge, Alex," the girl with the mousey hair said.

"Eugenia, she's new," Alexis returned, "Why don't you just shut up?"

Eugenia. Emma shut the door. She would remember that name, too. *Eugenia.* Obviously, all the girls there weren't as nice as Alexis.

Another ten minutes passed. Emma sat on the bed and waited in her robe.

A knock. That surprised her, that anyone there would knock. Well, she felt Alexis probably would, "Come in," she said.

A woman entered carrying several plastic bags and several suits of clothing on hangers.

Emma recognized her, "You're the one who yelled at that guy who was hurting me…you're *Heather*?"

"Yes, and there was no reason for him to be treating you the way he was, although, Emma—"

"You know my name." Emma felt certain she had found another friend.

"Yes, I know your name, but you'll be given another name."

"Why?"

"*Emma* is too…"

"Too nice?"

Heather smiled, "Something like that." Heather then laid the clothes on hangers carefully on the bed and spread them out, then handed her two bags, "Here, you'll find everyday underclothes in here, which is what you'll wear now, and in this bag other regular clothes, also what you'll wear now."

"*Now…?*"

Heather didn't answer, and didn't smile, "Just get dressed, Emma." She then set the other bags in the corner, and hung the clothes in clear plastic in the closet.

Emma's heart sunk. She felt sure they were going to be mean to her again and she didn't know how much more she could take, and she had felt sure that this woman was going to be a friend, and would help her…but she wasn't being very friendly. So she dug through the bags, found panties, bra, socks, then jeans and a top.

"That's good," Heather said, "Get dressed."

"What about shoes?"

Heather pointed, "Wear your shower shoes."

"Why can't I have real shoes? Those two awful people who brought me here took my other shoes!"

Emma noticed that Heather blinked at the words '*awful people*' and wondered why? Had she struck a nerve? She suspected that Heather in some dark and far back past had been brought into this business the same as her, and that she agreed with the words '*awful people*'.

But not enough, "Because with shoes you might try to run away, Emma. Barefooted, with snakes and rocks out there, not so likely. Now get dressed."

Emma got dressed but her heart again was sunk, and her stomach felt completely empty.

"Let's go," Heather said, opening the door and gesturing. Emma went through and into the area where the other girls waited, and were looking at her. She looked for Alexis. Alexis was there but not looking at her. They all must have known what was coming. Far in the back of her mind, Emma knew too, but refused to think about it.

"You're gonna get your little ass burned now, baby,"

Eugenia said, and then got pushed off her chair by Alexis.

"That's enough, girls!" Heather said, then waved to someone outside.

A man entered. Emma stared at him but did not see a human being, just someone who likely would do what he was told, *whatever* he was told.

"Alexis and Eugenia need a refresher on what goes on here," Heather said.

Emma threw her hand to her mouth. She wanted to protect Alexis and did stare at her, but Alexis shook her head negatively, barely, but enough to warn Emma not to say anything and not to get involved at all.

Heather pointed at the door, "Let's go, Emma."

****

They didn't go far, just to the building next door. Emma heard a couple slaps and screams come from the house, but certainly they wouldn't hurt those girls, at least wouldn't hurt them so much that bruises would show. Even Emma thought she understood that much.

At the door Heather stopped, "I won't be going in with you, Emma—"

"But you're the only nice one!"

Heather blinked. Emma was certain she had struck another nerve but also was certain it would do no good. Heather was as locked into this world as anyone else.

"I have some things to tell you, Emma." Heather went on, "In case you haven't figured it out yet, you are going to be a prostitute, a well-paid one. Yes, they're going to pay you, but they keep the money in savings for you—" Emma felt that was hard to believe, but didn't interrupt. "But prostitution is a hard life. You just heard from the house what happens if you don't do what you're told and *worse* can happen." Heather didn't elaborate, but Emma was pretty sure what '*worse*' meant. "In here, now,"

Heather pointed, "You're going to receive your final training session. It's…what some men want, and pay well for. After today you either will be a high-paid, high-end, prostitute, or, you won't. Emma, honey, in there I suggest you do exactly as you're told." Heather pointed and nodded.

****

When Emma left that building it was already dark. She was glad of that. She didn't want anyone to see her, or touch her, or even speak to her. She hoped all the other girls would be gone, even Alexis. She didn't even want to see Alexis.

But almost nobody was gone. They all waited in the same room. She wondered if that was the only place they ever spent time…maybe so. Maybe it was the only place they had. No game room probably, where they could put puzzles together or play checkers. She almost wanted to laugh…*almost*. And they all looked at her, but nobody showed any sign of wanting to torment her, not even Eugenia, who immediately looked down. None of the girls met her eyes. She almost wished somebody would say something—anything!—so she could go and bash that person, but nobody did.

Then her eyes met Alexis, and Emma lost it. The choking sobs began even before she could turn away and run into their room. Alexis came in right behind her, closed the door, and threw her arms around her. Alexis of course knew what had just happened to her. Obviously they all did, and Emma was so glad Alexis had come to her. She turned to her and buried her face in Alexis' front. "Cry, Emma, it'll help a little."

And Emma did cry, as silently as she could, as she didn't want the other girls to hear, but did feel they would understand.

"Let's lie down, Emma, they won't bother you again until at least tomorrow."

"OK." Emma moved to the bed but didn't hardly let go of Alexis, and Alexis held onto her too. Eventually they lay facing each other. Emma felt a little embarrassed being so, intimately, close to another girl, but at the same time she wanted and needed that closeness, for when she left that other building she was feeling absolutely no good emotion. Only anger, anger so violent that she felt she could have killed someone, *anyone*, if she would have had a chance, so, yes, she needed this body-on-body closeness, "Alexis, what did that girl, Eugenia, mean when she said '*taste*'?

"It's how we're required to live, Emma." Alexis relaxed her hug and leaned back.

"No! Keep holding me, please!"

So Alexis moved back into the gratifying hug, "All we have for love, Emma, for real, honest, love, is each other. All the girls sleep together, just like you and I will, in the same bed because each room only has one bed. But some of the girls not only sleep together but also make love together, and Emma, I haven't done that. I've had two other roommates, but I haven't done that. I haven't really wanted to, yet, but, if one of them would have *wanted* to…well, I don't know what I would have done. It would have been hard to say '*no*'."

"What happened to your roommates?"

"I don't know. I think they just moved to one of the other houses. The first one and I got too friendly and they separated us. I'm not sure about the other."

This time Emma moved back and really looked at her new roommate, "I have never done that either, Alexis, I mean, make love with another girl...? I…I, haven't even ever thought about it…."

"I'm just telling you this, Emma, so that you know what goes on here, and that, if, you ever wanted to…well, I've only known you a few hours, but I would never reject you."

Spontaneously, they both pulled back into the hug, and they held, for several minutes, finally, "Those men were so cruel, Alexis. How could they be so cruel? Have they never held and loved a child? Has a woman never loved and held them? Even when they were children, did anybody ever, *ever*, love them?" Emma snuggled even closer to Alexis, "There were three. First they all did what they wanted while the others watched. It…it became like a game to them. Sometimes they acted like innocent little boys just trying something for the first time, then they changed back into the cruel men that they are. Over and over and over, Alexis, they never stopped! They never asked if I was OK, or if I wanted to rest, they just kept…raping me!"

Emma snuggled even closer and began to sob again, quietly, and Alexis held her and held her, "I'm here for you, Emma."

"It just went on and on and on, like a nightmare that you just couldn't wake up from. When they all finished—at least I *thought* they were finished—one said, '*Just stand there, and let us look at you*'. I thought about covering myself, but…" A strong sob burst from her. She choked, and buried her face in Alexis' front, and hair, "So they just *looked* at me and began discussing who was going to do what during, as they put it '*the finale*'. They just *talked* about my body as if…as if…." The sobs burst forth again, strong ones. Emma could not stop them.

"Emma, you don't have to tell me anymore. I know what they did, because they did it to all of us. They were college boys, right?"

Between sobs, "Yes. I think so."

Alexis spoke strongly, obviously getting out her emotions too, "And they're always different boys. They're paid to come out here and do this to us, and they're required to ride in the back of the van too, so that they don't know where we are, or how to get to us." Alexis stopped for a few seconds, and took a breath, "They use these young boys because they know college boys are not only horny but full-of-it! They can go on and on with little rest!" Again Alexis took a breath, "I don't really blame the boys, Emma, I mean, they're boys! They can't help themselves! And I know *all* boys wouldn't do such a thing. But the fact remains, Emma, the boys who were out there today, and all the boys before them… they all had a choice. But they chose to do what they did."

The two girls snuggled together even closer, if that was possible, but neither felt any embarrassment about it. And Emma felt safer and more protected than she had for a long time. In fact, the last time she had felt so safe was with her mom and her mom's boyfriend, before he disappeared, and again that long ago memory of a man had intruded into her thoughts. But she resolved to keep him in the back of her mind. If he thought all that was necessary was to send birthday cards, then even if he knew of her plight he wouldn't come. *Nobody* was coming for her! She needed to accept that. If she ever would be free again she would have to do it herself. She needed to accept *that* too.

****

The next day at about five o'clock, the last person Emma ever hoped to see again arrived. Emma and Alexis were in their room when the woman who had accompanied Fletcher during their trip from Montana, arrived, the woman who had violated Emma worse than any of the men, simply because she *was* a woman, who should have protected Emma, but didn't.

"Well, little sweetums, good to see you again. Alexis, you can leave."

Alexis got up quickly and left. Emma watched Alexis leave, and felt her time had finally come. The woman shut the door, then, "Tonight you get to put to work all that good training we've given you."

Emma said nothing.

"Not going to talk, huh? That's OK. I'll talk for both of us." She walked to the closet and started examining the clothes in the clear wraps, and took down a black piece, then held it up to Emma, whose thought was to step away but she thought better of it. Then the woman looked in the bags that Heather had brought the day before, and brought out a short silk slip, and '*Barely There*' panties and bra, everything black, and gazed back at Emma.

"Get undressed, sweetums, and put these on." The woman laid everything on the bed, then opened her purse, "Oh, yes, your date tonight wants you to wear stockings and a garter belt too." She removed the items from her purse and laid them with the rest on the bed. "You're going to be dressed fit to kill, sweetums."

Emma's fists were tight, and she had not yet moved.

"If you're waiting for me to leave, forget it. Now get those rags off and get these

beautiful clothes on."

Emma still didn't move. The woman reached into her purse again and removed a long piece of…it looked like leather.

"This is a type of whip, sweetums. If I were to use it on say your legs, or your back, or your stomach—just to name a few places—it would leave a red welt. The welt would soon disappear, but the sting would stay for awhile. I guess there's some chemical involved that's been made part of the leather, an actual ingredient." The woman pulled the whip through her fingers, "It won't come off on me though, it needs to be struck…."

Emma decided she could not fight this woman, but someday she would. In the next minute she removed every stitch of her clothing.

The woman stopped her, "Turn around, sweetums."

Emma did as told.

"Oh, you are one beautiful little girl. I hope they didn't hurt you too badly yesterday, did they?"

"No." She wouldn't tell this cruel woman even if they had.

"Good. Because if you don't work out for our boy-customers…I might just take you for myself…."

Good. I will kill you in your sleep!

"You may dress now, sweetums, but do it slowly. I want to enjoy you this first time."

Emma felt so repulsed at the implications of this woman that she wanted to scream! But she was learning, learning what she had to know to survive, and to escape. She first put on the bra. It fit, and held her breasts comfortably. And she heard the sigh from the woman before her. She wanted to kick her! Then the bikini panties that she also filled comfortably, and which also brought another sigh, and request, "Please turn around again, sweetums."

She did, and stiffened herself so her lower back arched which caused her buttocks to flare slightly, something she had learned in gymnastics. It had the desired effect and brought another sigh from the woman watching her, and again Emma wanted to kick her! But Emma was learning that she did have some power over the woman.

"All right, dear, you may continue dressing. And, by the way, my name is Fleurette."

Emma didn't think she liked the name change, but it did tell her of her power. Because she had exposed herself, sexually, the woman, *Fleurette*, had softened. Someday, if she had the chance, she would use that power. She then sat on the bed and began pulling on the stockings.

"The stockings have seams, dear. Someone your age probably wouldn't know about too much, but some of our older clients love those seams on the backs of their ladies' legs, but don't worry. If you have trouble I'll help you."

As Emma finished pulling on the second stocking she noticed the woman putting the whip back into her purse. The second stocking on she then picked up the garter belt, stepped into it and pulled it up to ride on her hips.

"Let me help you, dear." The woman set her purse down and approached, "Just turn around and I'll hook you up."

Emma turned, and cringed as she felt the woman's hands grazing her while fiddling with the garter snaps. Both garters were snapped. Emma started to turn, but the palm of a hand on her inner left thigh between her panties and the top of her stocking stopped her. She actually flinched. She could not help it.

"Ah, I see you're still a bit touchy, sweetums, but you'll get over that." The woman, *Fleurette*, left her hand where it was and very slowly moved it upward, and stopped just before reaching her crotch. Emma's eyes were closed so tight and her fists clinched so tightly they almost hurt. Fleurette then removed her hand from Emma's inner thigh and put both hands on the outsides of her hips, and turned her. The hands on the outsides of her hips caused Emma little emotion, so she unclenched her fists. "I know that bothered you, dear, but, really, I didn't hurt you, and, if you just would allow yourself to relax, you might come to like it…and to like *me*."

I will never like you!

But the implication of what Fleurette really wanted was there, in living color and flashing lights, and, in the back of her mind, Emma began considering it as a way to escape. Fleurette then snapped the other two garters, took a good long look at Emma's middle and then stood, and backed away, and smiled, but it was not a warm and wholesome smile, "You're very beautiful, dear, I'd like to fuck you right here and now."

You already have, you bitch!

Fleurette handed Emma the slip. Emma put it on. It reached far enough to cover the tops of her stockings, but barely, then the dress, at least three layers of gauzy material. It covered a little more than the slip. Finally the shoes. Glitzy, extra-high-heels. It would be only the fourth time Emma had worn anything but flats. She hoped she could balance herself, but somehow suspected she wouldn't be doing much walking.

"OK, sweetums, you're dressed and the van is loading, so get your little ass out there."

Strange how the woman could go from '*dear*' to '*sweetums*' so quickly. Just one more method of control she guessed. Emma opened the door, walked through the sitting area, noticed the only girl there was Eugenia, wondered why, for about two seconds, then stepped through the outside door and closed it quickly. She had felt that awful woman's eyes on her all the way through the house. Halfway to the van she felt the eyes on her again.

At the van they didn't even provide a stepping stool. She would have to lift her dress to step up, and totally expose herself, but she figured the other girls would have had to do it too. She looked in. No, of the four girls already there only one wore a short dress. *To hell with it!* She lifted her dress, stepped up, grabbed the bolted down seat and pulled herself in.

Two men sat in the front seats. A third man crawled in back and closed the back doors, but didn't lock them. Emma noticed that. If the man didn't block her she was sure she could get out the back and run. Not tonight, though, given how she was dressed, and Alexis, sitting way up in front would never make it. But when they were alone she would mention it to Alexis. The third man—an older man maybe not so physically able to run—of course, sat down next to Emma and pushed her over. So no way she could get past him. She looked again for Alexis. Not that far away, but no place open beside her, and she doubted anybody would change seats, and she doubted it was very far to town. She and Alexis' friendship would just have to wait for privacy. Just one more thing she would have to accept...for now.

****

The van stopped. The man sitting in the passenger seat looked back and gestured. The man beside Emma opened the back door, jumped out, grabbed Emma's arm and jerked her out. Emma landed on those high heels and almost fell down and chanced a glance back at Alexis, who sent her an encouraging look. The passenger man was out nearly as quickly and jerked out the girl Emma had sat by. Then the four were in the hotel back door, so quickly that nobody outside could have seen them.

Next they reached an elevator, the *freight* elevator, Emma noticed. So they were just freight to these cruel people. Each little thing Emma learned hardened her, but the thought of what was still coming frightened her even more. It horrified her, and appalled her more than anything. The man kept his hold on her arm and pulled her quickly along, even as she kept turning her ankle. He stopped, "Take'em off if you can't walk in'em!"

She did, and she felt a frightened whimper leave her—yes! She was frightened of these people. She kept trying to be brave but knew she wasn't, and she had nothing to fight with, but at least now she could walk, and keep up. They reached a door and stopped. The other pair stopped at a door right across the hall. The man kept a tight grip on her arm and inserted a key. The door opened. He pushed her inside, then joined her, "Your name is Trudy. Your date tonight is fifty-six years old. You *will* do anything he tells you to do. If you don't he will tell us, and that will be bad news for you. And don't even think about running away. We don't own the hotel but we do own this section of this floor, and the doors and elevators all require keys. "

She hadn't noticed him use a key in the elevator. She had been too frightened to notice everything.

"Am I understood?"

"Yes, sir." Emma felt so small she wanted to disappear.

"When your date comes he will use his own key to unlock the door. He expects you to be waiting for him and fully dressed. And put your heels back on! Any questions?"

"No, sir." Again Emma felt small, so insignificant that she could run and jump through the window and kill herself, and nobody would even know she was gone. She had never in her life felt so low. She put her heels back on. They felt better.

The man left. The door closed. Now just to wait. She looked at the window. It was strong, and had many metal joints. No way to break it even with a hammer, she'd need a hacksaw, and no way to get out anyway. They were too far above the street. If she jumped she would get hurt but she probably wouldn't die. And right that moment she *wanted* to die. Where was her mom's boyfriend? She wished that man's memory would leave her. She hated him! She wanted to scream!

Time passed. Emma's mind went from the far past to a future she held out little hope for right then, a future of playing tennis professionally and for fun counseling runaway girls, like herself, except she hadn't ran away, but she had thought about it, many, many, times. Then her mind went deep into the past, to a favorite time with her mom's boyfriend. She didn't remember if it was before her mom's death, or after, but it didn't matter. She was happy with her mom's boyfriend. The dinosaurs had come to town to town. Huge, moving beasts controlled by remotes, and they moved like they were alive. Even baby dinosaurs, and after the show there were rides on the smaller ones and her mom's boyfriend had allowed her to ride on each one! Oh how she loved that day, and how she loved Mom's boyfriend—and then he was gone. And he never came to see her or called her—he just sent stupid birthday cards! *I hate him!*

Tears almost came, and would have, but a key in the door sobered her. And again she had to force her feelings away. But she would. She could. It was time, to act, to pretend she wanted to do this, to do anything this man would want. The door opened. A man came in. Not a big man. Not fat, not skinny, not bald, not anything, just a man wearing a suit, "Hello there," he said, then he smiled. It wasn't a bad smile.

Emma didn't think she could hate him, so she answered, "Hello." Her voice didn't crack. She had feared it would, but she sounded fine, as if she were just meeting a new teacher for the first time. That's what she thought of right then, but this wasn't a teacher.

The man closed the door, and locked it. She heard a click! Why would he lock it? What did he want?

"Come here, sweetheart."

I'm not your sweetheart! But she went anyway, of course, now walking easily in her high heels. She had learned well, and quickly.

The man reached inside his suit coat. Emma stopped, staring. A knife appeared. Its blade flicked out with a loud click! "Trudy, come here." The man's smile kept on.

Who's 'Trudy'? Emma's breath left her. Then she remembered. *She* was '*Trudy*'. But why a knife?

"Come *here*!" The man kept smiling, at least kept his face twisted in what he must have thought was a smile, but it wasn't a smile. Emma knew she could not run from him. She couldn't escape. She might as well let him kill her if that's what he wanted.

She approached him, and waited.

"Now, that's a good girl." The smile, the *truer* smile, was back. "Lift up your dress!"

She obeyed. She lifted her dress, and waited.

He dropped to his knees. His left hand gripped her right hip. Emma's eyes closed but she saw the knife moving toward her. No use watching. He would shove it into her and she would die. She would bleed all over herself, and him, and the floor, and she would die and be done with this awful life. She felt her panties grabbed, then felt the cold blade on her upper leg, then a jerk, then another, then her panties left her. She felt the draft of air between her legs…she was naked. No more modesty they said. She didn't care. She opened her eyes. The man remained there on his knees, looking at her. Maybe that's all he wanted, just to look at her. She could handle that, but knew he would soon want more, and whatever he wanted she would give to him, *whatever* the hell he wanted!

"Get on the bed," he said, "Leave your shoes on, leave everything on!"

Emma moved to the bed and sat down, and waited.

"Lay down, sweetheart."

Again Emma did as she was told. With her dress she covered herself as much as possible, not that it mattered, and waited. She no longer was afraid of him. She felt he just wanted her panties off, that he had not meant to frighten her. She felt he maybe was just shy. She knew some men never got over being shy. Hell, some girls too, and she knew she herself was shy. She wouldn't look at him though, so she put her eyes on the ceiling, but began to wonder what was happening. Did he want her to encourage him? And if she didn't would he tell on her? That she didn't make him happy? And then they would beat her, maybe? Or kill her? Should she speak to him? Is that what he wanted? He didn't frighten her anymore, so she began to feel she *should* encourage him, "Sir…?" She turned her head. The man was still on his knees, "Sir…don't you want me…?" She felt very strange offering herself to him, but she didn't know what else to do.

Then came a loud knock at the door! Then a key, and a click! Then in came a second man, "Waldo! You dumb fuck! What're you doing on the floor?"

Waldo held up Emma's panties, "Look! I got'em!"

The second man was larger, taller, more frightening, "Take the panties, Waldo, if that's all you want, and get the hell out of here!"

Waldo did as he was told. Emma heard the door close and kept still, now looking at the ceiling again, not knowing what to do but knowing there was nothing to do but wait.

"Well, baby, you probably thought you were going to get an easy night with that dumb fuck, didn't you?"

She felt the bed move, and knew he was coming. She closed her eyes. She would just let him do what he wanted and then he would leave...sometime...sometime he would leave. She knew that and hoped that, so she would just wait, and do what he wanted, whatever he wanted.

The bed moved even more. Emma clenched her fists and kept her eyes closed. The man pulled her right leg to open her, then pushed her other one, and grabbed her dress and slip and threw them up. She was naked. This is what men wanted. They wanted to see women naked, especially young women. She felt him staring at her for a long time, but he didn't stop like Waldo did...Waldo, what a funny name, Waldo, it reminded her of something, but she couldn't think of what.

The bed began to move again. She knew he was preparing himself. Then she felt his hands on the bed beside her, and she began smelling his alcoholic breath as he crawled over her...*no*... how stupid to think '*no*' she couldn't stop what was happening to her—

She felt his weight come down on her. At the same time she felt his...she couldn't even *think* the word! Even in the privacy of her mind she couldn't bring herself to say the official name of that private part of a man—she felt his huge thing enter her, then a few gentle thrusts, surprising her, then harder and faster, almost-out-of-control-thrusts, then his release and much grunting, and then his collapse on her, and then quiet. He had lasted about one minute—what a total weenie-ass! It crossed her mind to laugh, but she didn't dare laugh. He was asleep! He must be! Maybe drunk and passed out. But she couldn't move. He was too heavy, and if she moved he might awaken and hurt her, and tell on her, that she didn't do everything he wanted. Was that what he wanted? Did he just want her to lie quietly beneath him till he woke up again? What if he peed in her? She knew she would start screaming and not be able to stop, but screaming would do no good. Those awful people own this part of the hotel. Nobody would come to help her.

She whimpered, and became furious at herself for her whimper, for her weakness! So she would do it! She would just lie there quietly until he woke up! She felt her sanity slipping. How could she go on living like this? And letting stupid men do what they want with her, as if she were a plaything! She felt so angry! She wanted to scream! *Mom! Oh, Mom, I miss you so much—and where is your stupid boyfriend? Why doesn't he come and help me? Why does he think sending birthday cards are enough? They aren't enough! They aren't! They just AREN'T!*

Even in the privacy of her own mind Emma couldn't bring herself to say her late mom's boyfriend's name. She *knew* his name, she had not forgotten, but his name stayed way, way, far in the back of her mind with the growing-vague memory of her mother. And if she never saw him again eventually memory of that name would disappear too. Maybe next year if he sent her another stupid birthday card she would return it *'addressee deceased'*. That would show him—she wanted to scream! She just wanted to SCREAM!

****

Bailey Forbes could see her in the distance. And she saw him. The aunt. Had he seen her earlier he would have tried to avoid her, but she saw him first, smiled, and waved. It wasn't that Bailey disliked her—well, somewhat, maybe—but he simply saw no reason for a lot of communication with her, because…well, she had taken from him the only thing he cared about, the only thing he loved, the only thing that had once made his empty life worth living. At least she had seen to it that he lost it. Somehow the aunt had to have been at fault, but Bailey wasn't sure anymore. A lot of time had passed.

The aunt's smile remained as she approached, but somehow it didn't seem sincere, and disappeared when she arrived. Evidently she just couldn't keep it starched on, "She's gone," she said.

Bailey felt dumbfounded, "That doesn't tell me much, Evelyn. Who's gone? And gone where?"

"Emma. And I don't know where."

Now he felt a little angry, but kept it under control, "Come on, Evelyn, you must know *something*."

"I don't."

"When was the last time you saw her?"

"A month ago."

"A *month*! Good Christ! And what do you mean, gone? Did she run away? Abducted—*what*? And you didn't think I would want to know?"

"I didn't know. I haven't seen you for years, you know. I haven't ever heard from you. I don't even know where you live… and I don't have your number."

"I send cards every year, Evelyn. You see that Emma gets them, don't you?"

"Of course I do."

"And anyway, I haven't moved, and I have the same number, and it's not like we've exactly been friends. What happened? Why did she leave? You must know that, or at least have an idea."

"I think it might have been Merle—"

"Your boyfriend?" He had heard they were divorced; he should have tried to get in touch with Emma then; he was an idiot! "That prick is your boyfriend again?"

"Yes."

"Well, goddamn it, what do you think happened?"

"I don't know, Bailey." Evelyn's manner changed as her hand went to her mouth, "Emma had been moody—moodier than usual—and, the day before she left she seemed to be in an awful mood."

"All right. When, exactly, did she leave?"

"November 9th. I remember it was raining that day. She went out to do her cleaning and never came back." Evelyn reached her hand to Bailey's left shoulder, squeezed for one or two seconds, then withdrew, "That's all I know, Bailey."

"Merle working?"

"Yes, *when* he's working, at Ruark's Ironworks again…he might be off tonight all ready, but he never gets home till late."

"Does he still hang out at Kelly's?"

"Yes, but he's got lots of friends there."

"Friends, right. I'll check, Evelyn, and do *not* call him."

"I won't."

Bailey shook his head, lifted his hand in farewell, and started away. "And don't worry. He won't hear it from me that you told me anything."

Evelyn shook her head in response, "Yeah, right, who the hell else would tell you?"

"So call him then. Tell him I beat it out of you. Tell'im whatever the hell you need to protect yourself, Evelyn, because I probably won't be around for awhile to help you…should you need help."

Evelyn's last words surprised him, "Find Emma, Bailey, and bring her home."

****

Kelly's was the only bar in Industrial Park. Kitty-corner a half block from the front door, Bailey stepped into an alley and waited. Two cars and an older pickup were parked nearby, more in back he suspected. Little chance to get in without Merle seeing him and getting his pals around him. Maybe if he went to the back and waited near the restroom.

Unfortunately he had never been inside Kelly's, as the redneck atmosphere just didn't suit him. Likely it suited Merle quite well. So the back door it would be.

Bailey retraced his steps, crossed the street, noticed a third car arrive but didn't recognize the occupants, then looked for his own car a block away. Out of sight, but still there, of course. He knew he might need a quick getaway, as he had never stalked someone before. He also had never threatened someone before, had never had a real fight. He had no training whatsoever for what might be about to occur. Even those eight years in the army he had received no real combat training. As a stateside stock clerk he probably didn't have to know how to kill. Maybe should have volunteered, as those years were plenty boring. So he would just have to learn. But maybe Merle would be friendly, maybe would tell him whatever he needed to know and he would have Emma back home in a jiffy. Yeah, and maybe the world truly was a bowl of cherries.

Behind the bar, yes, more parked cars. He reached the back door. The handle felt cold, and sticky, maybe even slimy, like the world he was about to enter. He turned the knob. The door came open. Mostly darkness poured out. He slipped in and closed the door, then waited for his eyes to adjust to the dim light, and saw a vague hiding place and reached it just before the bar door opened and a small amount of light came in. And of all people: Merle, who then entered the restroom.

Bailey gave him thirty seconds, enough time to get his business out by the urinal, then he too entered the restroom and locked the door. It clicked. Merle, busy with his business, appeared not to even notice the sound. "So how's Evelyn?"

Merle continued with his business but did look up and back, "Who the hell are you?"

"You don't remember me. That's cool, Merle, but hurtful. What about Emma? How's she?"

Merle finished with his business, shook off, zipped up, turned around, "What do you know about Emma? And how the hell do you know my name?

"I know you, Merle, and I'm asking, how's Emma?"

"I don't know." Merle was about an inch shorter than Bailey's 5'10", but a good 20-30 pounds heavier. His head was big, his face big, and somewhat elongated with big, fleshy lips, which tightened, then opened, "Haven't seen her."

"I think you're lying, Merle. You maybe were the last person to see her."

"Bullshit! She...probably was out cleaning...!"

"Whose house was she cleaning?"

"I don't know! How the fuck should I know whose house she was cleaning?"

"She lives with you and Evelyn, Merle. You should know something about her."

"I don't!"

"You idiot, Merle. I could never see what the hell Evelyn saw in you." Bailey took a step forward.

Merle backed up, into the sink, "What the hell do you want, anyway?"

"I want to know what you know."

"I don't know anything!"

"Who knows then? Somebody knows something Merle, and you know who."

"OK! Like I said, she was cleaning house for some guy. He came home early and wanted her little ass and she fought him...."

"And...?"

"And fightin' didn't help. He got his piece of her."

"Emma told you this?"

"No. *He* did. Braggin' about it all over the bar that night.

"What night? How long ago?"

"I don't know...."

Bailey advanced, "You're such an idiot, Merle, I think you do know."

Merle tried to step back, then moved sideways along the sinks, "About a month ago—Christ! I don't know!"

"The guy's name, Merle...."

"Jackson. What the hell, he's right out there in the bar."

That kind of changed things. Bailey wasn't ready to try facing down two guys, and he had no idea about Jackson, "Let's go out there, Merle. Introduce me."

Merle's mouth fell open, "Christ...."

Bailey pointed, "Let's go. You stay in front of me."

****

The main bar wasn't much brighter than the restroom. Merle pointed at a man about six feet tall standing at the close end of the bar, who tipped a beer back and finished it, "That's Jackson. I don't know his first name, or maybe that *is* his first name."

"Introduce us."

"Christ, you're crazy."

"Do it."

"It's your funeral." Merle grinned, then turned away, "Hey! Jackson!"

"Yo!" The man looked up, grinned at Merle, then sent his eyes to Bailey, giving Bailey a strange sensation that the man didn't exactly know him, but somehow knew what he wanted. The grin disappeared as Jackson slammed his empty bottle on the counter, then turned away, shouted, "More beer!"

Merle took a position at the foot of the bar, about four feet away, "Jackson, this here's Bailey Forbes. He wants to meet you, and join your fan club...."

Jackson, holding onto the empty bottle with his left hand, dark eyes steady and unsmiling, stepped up and extended his right hand, "Hey, Bailey. How the hell are ya?"

"I'm OK, Jackson." Bailey grasped the hand, and felt a grip he likely wouldn't be able to break easily, should he need to, "Understand you like young girls...."

"That's correct. I like breakin' them in, and I really like them tender young inner thighs...bout the softest and smoothest thing this side of heaven." Jackson relaxed his grip, stepped back to the bar as his beer arrived, and hung onto the empty in his left hand. The eyes didn't change.

Bailey didn't know what to do next, or say, but something came out anyway, "So what young girl did you last break in?"

"I believe her name was Emma...and, as I recall, I believe Merle here said she was eighteen. So it's not like I did something wrong." Jackson turned away.

"When?"

"I remember cause it was my birthday. November 9. And what a great present that little girl gave me." Jackson hung onto his empty and did swing his gaze back, "Now, I'm gettin' a bit tired of visiting with you, new member of my fan club. So, if you don't want your ass kicked I'd leave."

"I'll leave, but a question first. Was the present she gave you consensual? Or did you just take it from her?"

Jackson kept up his gaze. His eyes narrowed, "She loved it. She begged for more, but, hey, I get what I want and then I'm done." He laughed, "Time for rest."

"Right, I doubt that a lowlife like you has the staying power to actually *please* a woman." Bailey heard Merle gasp. Jackson stayed steady but his hand did tighten on his beer bottle. Time to leave, "It does seem like you were about the last person to see her, though, Jackson…." Bailey waited for a possible answer, or comment, then headed for the front door, "Oh, and nice visiting with you too."

****

Heading for his own car, Bailey decided the blue and white older Ford pickup truck parked in front of the door was likely owned by Jackson. He figured Jackson knew something more about Emma, but wasn't quite sure what to do about it. He was considering something, something that a TV hero would do, would *get away* with doing, that was, but if there wasn't a lot of choice involved…and approaching the law would likely be worthless. If the law could have helped Auntie Evelyn should have done it, and back when Emma first disappeared, a whole month ago.

Bailey reached his own car and entered it, and soon was turning the corner, which put him out of sight from the bar, then he quickly reached the next block, turned right and quickly went two more blocks, turned right again, went a half a block, then jumped out and hurried to the end of the block and peeked around the corner. The blue and white pickup had not moved. Bailey trembled. In mid-December it wasn't exactly warm in north-eastern Montana, and he wasn't exactly dressed for surveillance. Wasn't trained for it, either. In fact, if he made any mistakes in what he was planning to do he could get in a huge amount of trouble. But Emma was worth it. True, he had not seen her for years, but their bonding back when they *were* spending time together…well, he wasn't all that certain of their *mutual* bonding either. He had *thought* so, back then, yes, but things change, things happen. Yet, he couldn't get it out of his head that Emma not only needed him, but remembered him, everything, at least the important parts. And even if she *didn't* remember, he *did*.

The door to the bar opened. A head appeared, like maybe checking to see if the coast was clear. Then the man stepped out, closed the bar door and entered the blue and white pickup, and it pretty definitely was Jackson. Unfortunately, the pickup came down the street toward Bailey. He had to disappear, and had about two seconds to do it, and hadn't even considered that he might have to. What a detective he was! Wildly he looked around and saw a really scraggly evergreen bush against a chain link fence. He dived to it and was able to wedge himself in, just as the pickup came by. It slowed but didn't stop. And in his awkward position Bailey wasn't even able to look up and ensure himself that it truly was Jackson.

But he figured only Jackson would have felt like he should check at least this first block. When the pickup moved on Bailey rolled out and was able to get a full license number. Following the man, at least for then, was out. Definitely out, as the pickup slowed at the next block also, so very likely was Jackson wondering if Bailey was up to something. A day or two should pass. In the meantime, Bailey had a friend who used to be in law enforcement. With the license number he should be able to find out just about everything he needed to know about the man named Jackson.

****

Two days later Bailey had Jackson's home address and was waiting for him to arrive. He had an equalizer too, a Colt .45 semi-automatic pistol inside his jacket. But loaded with an empty clip. He didn't want to take the chance of accidentally shooting Jackson, or himself either. And, should he really need it, he had a loaded clip handy in his pocket. With the gun he felt pretty sure that Jackson would spill his guts…and speak of the devil.

The blue and white pickup turned into the driveway, and finally Bailey ensured himself that the driver definitely was Jackson. Surprisingly, considering the type of man he was, he lived in quite a nice house, and alone, and not likely with a wife. Nobody on record at least. And he had seen no other movement anywhere. Of course there was the possibility of a girlfriend sleeping inside, or soon getting off her shift. He didn't know, would go with what he did know.

The pickup stopped. Jackson got out and headed for the

back door. Behind a tree with a big trunk, Bailey made himself as small as possible. The instant Jackson had the door unlocked and pushed open Bailey made his move and stuck the Colt's barrel against Jackson's kidney and pushed, "Just step right inside, Jackson. Your fan club is about to meet."

Luckily, Jackson did as asked. Bailey followed, closed and locked the door and used the Colt's barrel to push Jackson further inside, "Don't turn around!"

Jackson took a couple hurried steps, "What the hell do you want?"

"I want to know what you know about Emma."

"I told you all I know, goddamn it!"

Bailey used the flat of his foot to push the back of Jackson's left knee first and then his lower back, hard. Bailey surprised himself at the moves, surprised mainly that they *worked*. Jackson sprawled into the room and landed prone on his side, facing Bailey, who now had the Colt aimed at Jackson's face, "Talk!"

"OK! Jesus!" Jackson covered his face and threw himself more to his right side, then, carefully, looked up, "What do you want to know?"

"Just start talking, Jackson. You got your birthday present, then what?"

"I sold her…."

Jesus! In the back of his mind Bailey had half expected Jackson's answer, but to actually hear the words almost sent him into a frenzy, but he kept control and approached and kept the Colt aimed, "You better remember a name…."

Jackson threw his hands over his face again, "Fletcher!"

"Fletcher-what?"

"Martin! Fletcher Martin!"

"Is he local?"

"I dunno!"

"Put your hands down, Jackson, I want to show you something."

Jackson lowered his hands. His eyes were big, more frightened then Bailey had expected. He then ejected the empty clip from the Colt, "This clip is empty." He slipped the empty into his shirt pocket and removed the other, and showed it to Jackson, "This one is fully loaded." He slammed it into the Colt's receiver, pulled the slide back and left it cocked, then held it up sideways and pointed to the cocked hammer, "I couldn't have shot you before, but now I can." He first released the hammer, then brought the Colt down into a solid point again, "Now speak, Jackson, everything you know about Fletcher Martin."

"He's not local! He…just appeared at the bar a while back and asked some questions."

"Like what?"

"Girls! He wanted girls!"

Bailey felt himself losing control and aimed the Colt at the ceiling, "Oh, God, I'm really losing patience with you, man—what else?"

"I told'im I knew of a hot little chick, then I told Merle to set it up for her to clean my house again. Martin said he had to go over to Lawson Springs but would be back in a week for her…."

Bailey shook his head, "You mutherfuckers—where'd he take her?"

"Vegas!" Jackson raised his hands again, "He takes his girls to Vegas!"

"You do this as a *business*?"

Jackson didn't answer.

"Fine, and in case you're considering charging me with assault, think of this. I could drag your ass to the cops right now, but that might affect my finding Emma, so I'm going to find her first."

Jackson just stared.

Bailey brought the gun back down to a point. He cocked it again, "God, I would love to shoot you right now!" He shook his head again, "I could just pull this trigger. You'd be dead and I soon would be hunted, and that wouldn't help Emma...."

Jackson covered his face again and pulled his body into a fetal position.

"I don't recommend that you warn Fletcher Martin that I'm coming, because if he hears from you, about me, and stops me from getting Emma back...well, I just don't recommend it, Jackson, cause then I'll be back to get you. Do we understand each other?"

Jackson gestured but didn't speak.

Bailey released the cocked hammer, then pressed the barrel against Jackson's head, "Goddamn it! I will come back, Jackson. I'll find you and I'll kill you!"

"All right! OK!" Jackson pulled himself into an even tighter fetal position, "Christ! I won't tell him!"

Bailey pulled the Colt up and retreated to the door. He saw no movement—wait! Movement! "There's a car pulling into your driveway—Who is it?"

"Christ, I don't know!"

"It's a small red car, newer...."

"I don't know!"

"Damn you, Jackson, get up!" Bailey pointed, "Who?"

"Jeeze, that's my girlfriend."

"Oh, great, and I doubted such a nice guy like you would even *have* a girlfriend. So get this, Jackson, I'm going to slip my gun inside my belt in back, just like the TV guys do it, and, believe me I can get it out fast. So, you introduce me like I'm a good friend of yours who was just leaving." He glanced outside. The woman was almost to the door. "Got it?"

"Got it."

Bailey stepped to the wall and slipped the gun into his belt in back, just as the outside door opened…*she must have her own key.* No surprise there he guessed.

She stepped in and looked at Bailey in surprise.

Bailey glanced at Jackson, then back at the woman who was staring at him.

"Hey, babe, this here's a good friend of mine…."

At Jackson's hesitation it occurred to Bailey that the man had forgotten his name, "Bailey, miss, Bailey Forbes." He stuck out his hand, "And you are?"

Still staring she glanced at Jackson, "I'm…Fleurette." She took his hand and gripped it, making Bailey wonder exactly what their relationship amounted to, as the woman—about forty, full head of rich brunette hair, just enough lipstick and eye shadow to make her gorgeous, with a gorgeous body to match—showed ten times the class of Jackson, and not *really* likely his girlfriend. So, what then? Business? Maybe the boss of the trafficking ring?

"Nice to meet you, Fleurette. Well, I was just leaving." He glanced at Jackson, "I will get back to you, my man."

A strange meeting. No way was Fleurette a girlfriend of Jackson, unless she was a pinnacle of low self-esteem… *Fleurette*…a feminine cover-name for *Fletcher…Fleurette* Martin? Possible. And if that was the case Jackson would be filling her in right now about Bailey Forbes, and maybe making plans to already move Emma. So he had to get to Las Vegas fast, though he had absolutely no idea what he would do once he got there. Not likely Fletcher Martin was listed in the phone book… but *Fleurette* Martin might be. He guessed the phone book would be at least a start.

Or maybe Fleurette really was Jackson's girlfriend. If Jackson were to clean up he maybe *could* be considered…one of the so-called *bad boys*: Dark, needing a shave, the kind even the most beautiful and sensible-looking women seemed to swoon over, so maybe he was wrong. He would remain open about that.

Should have asked Jackson if he was in touch with Fletcher Martin. Not likely, though, as Jackson likely was a pretty small operator, given the small town they lived in. Abundance, Montana, population 3600, probably had plenty of pretty girls the right age, but not so many that the adults wouldn't soon notice if quite a few started coming up missing. So Bailey's next move was finding the money to get to Las Vegas, and quickly.

****

"And what makes you think you'll even find her, Bailey?" Lance, Bailey's employer and close friend, both taller and younger, kept tightening the lug nuts on one of the chrome wheels of a 1974 Pontiac Firebird, and had made a good point.

"I don't know, my friend, but I have to try."

"And Las Vegas?" Lance grasped his air wrench and finished tightening down the lug nuts, "That's not a little town, Bailey, and, hey, isn't that where they film one of those CSI shows? You should contact them."

"Yeah, right."

"They always solve their crime, you know."

"I know," and he knew his friend was being silly, "The story takes place there, yes. But I don't know if they actually film it there, parts maybe. Anyway, I've been through Las Vegas, more than once."

"Yeah, riding a bus to and from army leave, but did you ever go exploring in that town? Visit any casinos, or cathouses?"

"No, no, and no…."

"Who *is* this girl, anyway? And how come I've never met her?"

"My foster daughter. When she and I and her mother were together she was very young. I had full plans to adopt her but her mother died, which sort of ended all our plans."

Lance shook his head, "You feel that close to her, huh?

OK, how much ya need?"

"Five hundred in cash, and another two thousand in my account."

"Just two?" Lance's brow raised, "This is Las Vegas we're talking about. Two thousand would be gone in about two minutes."

"Make it three then."

"I'll make it four, and you'll let me know if you need more, right?"

"Yes. I will."

"I'm serious, damn it, and what if you get in a real tight spot?"

"Then I'll give you a ring."

"And then I just close up shop and come down and get your ass, right?"

"Right."

"Yeah, right. How old is this girl?"

"She's eighteen."

"And how old when you last saw her?"

"Seven."

"And you think she'll remember you?"

"Doesn't matter if she does or not, cause I remember her…and, we bonded back then, so she'll remember."

"OK, my friend, let's go get your money."

****

Three hours later Bailey was airborne. His friend and employer had really come through for him, providing not only the $4500 but also a one-way ticket to Las Vegas. But Lance's face had taken on a different expression when Bailey handed over his Colt 45, "If I call on you, my friend, it will probably mean I'm in a lot of trouble, so you likely will need this. Better you bring mine than yours, and you have the concealed weapons permit."

"Not to go across state lines with, though."

"I've heard that's been changed, so that's something you can do some research for on the internet, during your long lonely evening hours."

"You do know I'm married…."

"Yeah, and I'm kidding, but just trying to get it across to you the kind of people we might have to go up against. And if you really want to see for yourself, visit Kelly's out in Industrial Park. Look up a guy named Jackson, and his sidekick Merle. A real pair of mothers' sons, those two."

"OK, Bailey, but we'll bank on the possibility you'll find this girl, she'll remember you and she'll *want* to leave whatever life she might have fallen into. What's her name, anyway?"

"Emma."

"Charming name. And that's how you're going to dress? A suit?"

"Just a casual black suit *coat*, my friend, the rest blue jeans and tennies."

And that's when they shook hands and gave each other the quick one-armed male hug and Bailey had run to be the last boarder.

He looked out the window. Nothing but white clouds. He had lucked out and gotten a window seat and nothing to look at but white clouds. But of course he wasn't exactly on a relaxing vacation. Something to look at besides white clouds would have been nice, though. Maybe a nap would help.

****

The giant aircraft's wheels hitting the tarmac woke Bailey. He had no idea how long he had slept, and no idea where he was. Didn't even know if his was a thru-flight. Some private detective he was turning out to be. He had no real plan at all, and he couldn't rent a hotel room. His money wouldn't last long that way. And great, landing at night, and he didn't exactly want to spend the night outside. Wait, he could spend a few hours right there at the airport, and figure out what to do in the morning.

So, he had at least the *beginning* of a plan.

Oh yes, and he could look at a phone book for the one name he had.

Once inside the receiving area though, there didn't seem to be many people. What? No night flights? That couldn't be. And all he needed was an immediate run-in with the law. Then he spied a restaurant. They probably sold ninety-dollar coffee, but that would be better than getting approached by airport security. Maybe could even ask some questions. But he had better hurry. As quiet as the place was the restaurant probably wouldn't be staying open long.

As suspected the restaurant was quiet too. Just one other patron. He sat at the counter. The waitress, a flawlessly-shaped brunette with her hair in a ponytail, about forty, came immediately, "What can I get ya?"

"First, are you open all night?"

"'Bout another half hour, then we're closed till four-thirty." She smiled.

"Fine, I'll have some black coffee, and a phone book." Bailey then noticed the wall clock. Only ten o'clock. Lord, he had the whole night to kill.

The waitress first brought the phone book. It didn't take long to look at the short page of Martins, but no *Fleurette* and, of course, no *Fletcher*. He closed the book and let go with a fairly loud sigh, just as the waitress brought his coffee, "You get one refill." She smiled again, and showed gorgeous white teeth, "Didn't find her, huh?"

"No." he let his knuckles hit the counter.

She kept her smile going but moderated it, "So, your first trip to Vegas?"

"It shows huh?"

She laughed, a gentle sound, "You could just as well have a sign around your neck, or maybe written on your forehead, saying, "I'm new in town. Please rob me, or scam me, or something, please…!" She laughed again.

Bailey laughed too, and didn't feel insulted. In fact this woman had easily slipped right under his skin. She now could do anything she wanted with him. Right, he definitely was a cool-headed private detective, "So help me understand Las Vegas."

"How can I help?" Her smile did not quit.

He began to suspect she might have a side job that got her much, much, more money than waiting tables. If he was wrong his question would be very insulting to her, might even get him slapped. But he would take the slap, no problem. He had to know, and hoped she really did want to help, "I do need some help, ah… with the shadier, darker, side of life here, but, well…are you, possibly, a hooker?"

Her warm smile disappeared and a real hurt look took its place. She walked quickly away.

Great start, Bailey, you completely idiot-dumbass! He put his hand over his face and rubbed down, and shook his head, and let out a breath. Again, what a great private detective he was turning out to be

The waitress had walked clear to the other end of the counter. The other customer then paid and left. Bailey hadn't even tasted his coffee yet, so he picked it up and carried it to where she stood, "I'm so sorry, miss…but I do need help, I honestly do."

"But if I was a hooker you wouldn't want my help, is that it?"

"No, I—I—thought—if you *were*—you would know something about that dark side of life—I, I'm trying to find my daughter!" He just blurted it out, "And now I don't know what else to say." He let out a held breath, "I'm just so sorry, miss, it's just that…well, you're very pretty—I mean, I'm not saying only hookers can be pretty—"

She touched his arm. The smile came back, "It's all right, sir. So, how can I help?"

"You would still help me?"

"Yes. Of course. Daughters are special. What's her name?"

"Emma."

Bailey noticed her reaction, if it *was* a reaction, probably wasn't.

"*Emma*. I love that name. My grandmother's name was *Emma Sue*."

So *that* caused the reaction. He decided to trust her, "First, will you please tell me your name?"

"Heather." She didn't even hesitate, and extended her hand, "And what's yours?"

"Bailey." He took hold of her hand. It was the warmest, softest hand he had held since Emma's mother died. The realization fully hit him then, that he had not allowed himself to truly appreciate another woman since that fateful day.

He wasn't sure how Emma would feel about him referring to her as his daughter, but, well, she possibly would never find that out. First he had to find her. He would worry later about the daughter thing. So he told Heather the whole story, and finished exactly at closing time, "So here I am, in Las Vegas without a clue."

"First, Bailey, you need a place to stay." She gave him the warmest smile yet, "And that will be with me—and don't worry, I won't try to seduce you. Anyway, you're not my type. Our arrangement will be, I'll feed you, and give you a room, and help you in any other way that I can. Our only goal is to find Emma."

****

Forty minutes later Heather guided her car into the driveway of an expensive-looking suburban home, in Bailey's mind a lot to pay for with what a waitress probably earned, but he wasn't about to suggest anything like that. He would get to know Heather in whatever way he could first. If he discovered any untruths, well, he would deal with that then.

She pushed a button on the dash and the garage door began opening. Once inside she pushed the button again and it closed. And that quickly they were in a very dark privacy. Bailey finally took the time to wonder exactly what he had gotten into. Then a light in the garage came on and Heather slipped her door handle, causing Bailey to do the same. Then he opened the back door and grasped both packages of groceries, and remembered Heather's comment, "I'm not used to men opening doors and pushing carts for me, not without my complaining, anyway."

"Well, I…," and he couldn't think what to say.

"Don't worry, Bailey." She touched his arm, "I'm not complaining about you either, and I can tell that you're the kind of man who just does things like that. I'm sure Emma's mother loved you deeply."

"Yes, I think she did."

Heather unlocked the door and held it open for Bailey, who set both packages down on a spotless and empty table, then went back for his one piece of luggage. Then he looked around. The room, obviously Heather's kitchen, also was spotless, and organized. A bowl of fruit sat on the cupboard, pots and pans and a cutting board hung from the wall close to a shining glass top electric stove…

"Are you hungry, Bailey?"

"I…wouldn't mind a cookie…."

A cookie jar sat next to the bowl of fruit. Heather pulled it close and opened it, "Chocolate chip cookies, just baked them last night."

Bailey helped himself to one, "Wow, you did that after work?"

"Yep, that's my easiest time for housework. Well, I'll

show you your room—"

The phone, on the wall by the garage door, rang. Heather snatched it up and answered in a quiet voice, then, "Please hold a sec, I have to put my milk away."

But she hadn't bought milk.

"Come on, Bailey, I'll get you settled in." She put her hand on his shoulder and guided him into a hallway, to a door probably the bathroom, and another that he expected was her bedroom. "You're right next to the bathroom here, and feel free to use whatever you need."

"Thank you, Heather." So his room would be right next to hers, but, of course, he couldn't think of anything *with* Heather, but the thoughts rolled through his mind anyway.

She waved and smiled and hurried back to the kitchen. Bailey wished he could hear the phone conversation, as his suspicion of "hooker" was back, but, what the hell? She had done nothing to lose his trust, and if she was a hooker, then she was. He pushed his one piece of luggage into the room, then entered himself and closed the door, and thanked his lucky stars for running into Heather. His good fortune was hard to believe.

About three quarters of an hour passed while he checked his luggage. He heard the shower running but thought nothing of that, then came a knock on his door, "Bailey…?"

"Yes…?" He opened the door. Heather stood there in a knockout dress, extra makeup, and her silky hair down. It graced her shoulders fabulously. *She's gorgeous.*

Her eyes…he couldn't tell what was in her eyes…not happiness for certain.

"I have to go out for awhile, Bailey."

He didn't know what to say, so just shook his head positively and said nothing. She closed the door. He heard her footsteps go down the hall, and waited for the sound of the garage door. It didn't come, but there was the sound of a car on the street. It stopped out front and he heard a car door close. Then it left.

Of course he didn't know what had just gone down and didn't especially like what he was thinking unconsciously, so refused to let the thoughts into his conscious mind. But maybe the reason Heather had so graciously offered to help with finding Emma was because she *did* have an inside line to that dark underworld. Time would tell. But another unconscious thought was filling the back of his mind, that once he got Emma out of whatever world she was in, he might just ask Heather to come out too. But those thoughts he really tried to keep out of his conscious mind.

****

Only about two hours had passed when Bailey was awakened by the sound of a car door, and then the side door leading to the garage, then the inside door from the garage, then footsteps in the hallway, finally a very, very, light knock on his door—that he didn't answer. The door opened and through slitted eyes he saw Heather enter his room and leave the door open to a dim light. Very quietly she walked to his bed, then stood there for a few seconds, and then sat on his bed, "Bailey…?"

"Yes…, Heather."

"What does Emma look like? You never described her."

"I haven't seen her for over ten years, but I know I would know her."

"I saw a girl tonight. She's about eighteen, and, yes, Bailey, I'm a hooker, one of the so-called high-end ones. That's how I can afford this house. It's even paid for. Are you angry with me? I didn't exactly lie, you know."

"I know. You just didn't answer, and absolutely *no*, I'm absolutely not angry with you. I would have no right to be angry." He reached for her wrist.

She turned her hand over and clasped his hand, then brought his hand to her face and pressed it against her cheek, then kissed his palm, "I can get you in, Bailey, but it'll cost you, a lot, and these are bad people. You could get hurt. They have guns, and people—even people I know personally—sometimes disappear.

Girls do too, if they get out of line, or try to escape. I think the only reason I'm still around is that by the grace of God I've somehow kept my looks. And there are some psychos out there who only want—" she used one hand to symbolize quotation marks, and kind of laughed, or, maybe, groaned, "—*older* women."

"You're very beautiful, Heather."

"She looked at him and smiled, and kissed his palm again, "Thank you. So you like—" she symbolized the quote marks again, "—*older* women too?"

"Well, if they're gorgeous, like you."

She looked at him and smiled again, "Like I told you before, Bailey, you're not my type...so there's no way I would do you without you paying."

"And I really don't have much money." He laughed, a little, "So, how would you get me in?"

"I don't know yet. We better sleep on it. I'll be out till at least noon. You can get up whenever you want and help yourself to whatever you want for breakfast, and I hope you won't go off half-cocked to look for Emma, because I guarantee you'll never find her by yourself."

"I won't, and I've always known I would need help, but I didn't expect to find help so soon."

"Right." Heather stood and started to go, then came back, leaned over and kissed Bailey very lightly on the cheek, "We'll make a good team, Bailey. I'm sure of it."

She had said, twice, that he wasn't her '*type*' but he felt he could change that if he tried. Time would tell.

****

The next morning early Bailey set about preparing his breakfast in Heather's very well-stocked kitchen, and was just sitting down to a plateful of over-medium eggs, crispy bacon, whole wheat toast, and orange juice, when in a flannel robe out came, "Heather, had I have known I would have made enough for you too."

"That's OK, Bailey." She walked past his chair, touched his shoulder and touched his cheek with her cheek—just a peck—then moved on to the cupboard and started preparing her own breakfast, "I didn't know when I'd wake up and rarely use an alarm, and, no, you didn't wake me."

Bailey's shoulder and cheek resonated from Heather's touch, making it a bit difficult to concentrate on his breakfast... *she said I'm not her type, twice she has said that.* He took a bite of bacon, then egg, then toast, began chewing in earnest and gazing at the woman moving about the kitchen in the most proper and modest outfit she could possibly wear, yet he saw her smooth body moving under the robe, could basically see no skin, but liked what he could saw...*not my type, not my type....*

She looked his way, and smiled. Bailey smiled back and let out a held breath.

"Today I'll show you the building she *works* in. Tonight, if I'm called—I'm not called every night—but if I am, I'll set a time for you to have sex with her—" Bailey felt his face change, drastically. "I know. That's not why you're here, Bailey. But you need to get your head wrapped around that concept. It's what she does. It's what she's required to do. She's required to perform whatever degrading sex act the man she's with that night wants from her. Yes, she can refuse, and likely in the beginning she attempted a few refusals. But a few beatings later one will do what they want. *Whatever* they want. That's why I used the word *sex*, Bailey. You have to get used to that idea, and it's the only way you'll get to see her, unless you think you can go in with guns blazing, like they do in the movies."

"No. I'm no hero...." *I've never been a hero, not to Emma, not to Emma's mother, not to anybody.* But at least he hoped to have a chance to try to make it up to her, "It's what happened to you too, isn't it?"

Heather didn't answer right away, then, "I'm sure—pretty sure—that some women enter prostitution and all the other parts of the sex trade, by choice, and I'm also pretty sure that most don't. They were molested at some young age, or abused in some other way, causing very low self-esteem for one thing, and when they get older they're enticed, somehow, then lied to, abducted and beaten and raped, and drugged, and many are plain murdered if they won't cooperate. Even your exotic dancers are pushed to start having sex for pay, and when they finally agree they're secretly filmed, then they're shown the video. If they don't want their family to see the video…well, you can imagine the rest."

Bailey knew Heather had just unloaded a lot of emotion. And, actually, he *couldn't* imagine. Even in the army he had not partaken of all the available avenues for sex. He almost felt embarrassed about his naiveté. He wasn't feeling naïve about Heather, though, and he wanted to hold her and tell her only good things. He also knew she wasn't ready to hear or do anything like that, with him. It was a good feeling though to have good feelings, again, about a woman—*not my type*. He couldn't get those words out of his mind, and knew the only way those words could get removed would be if Heather removed them herself, "I've got a friend I'd like to call, Heather. If the shit hits the fan, and I think it could, he would be a great help."

"Fine. Call him. By the way, it'll probably cost you a thousand, but for all night, which is what I'd recommend, it'll probably be two or three thousand—" Again Bailey felt his face change, drastically. "Are you good for it?"

"Yes, I just wasn't expecting…."

"I understand, and you *have* led somewhat of a sheltered life, haven't you?"

"Yeah, I guess so."

"It's because of her youth, Bailey, and if it's the girl I think, well, she's…special, which is what makes it so especially sad. A thousand is what I get too. Two thousand for all night. I no longer get *three* thousand, though."

"You should though, because you're special too."

"Thank you, Bailey." She looked at him for a few seconds, then gave him not such a big smile, "Now let's have our breakfast." Heather's breakfast turned out to be rather light, a blueberry muffin, skim milk, orange juice, coffee, "It's a little early in the day for me, Bailey. Had I gotten up at noon, as usual, I probably would have had something more like yours." She smiled, and sat down across from him.

Not my type. Fine. Bailey smiled back.

****

An hour later Heather pulled into a parking spot and pointed, "See that sign, Binghcon Hotel?"

Bailey stared, "Such a nice-looking building, and Emma actually *lives* there?"

"No, your little Emma is brought in when she's needed. And if you were to go in there and ask for her the desk clerk would look at you blankly. However, after you left he would make some quick phone calls with your description…."

"And…?"

"And…I don't know. As I said, people disappear."

"So where *does* she live?"

"That I won't show you, Bailey, because I don't quite trust you yet not to go in with guns blazing, although I wouldn't blame you if you did. The girls live together in guarded houses, out in the country, about three different houses that I know of."

"I thought prostitution was legal in Nevada."

"It is, but not in the counties where Las Vegas and Reno reside. How many other counties I don't know. But Las Vegas and Reno have your…high-rollers, so the *high-end prostitutes* are required. The pimps truck the girls in to certain places like the Binghcon Hotel. It's safer, and much easier, for the pimp, to keep the girls out in the country, especially if they aren't volunteers… like your little Emma."

Bailey couldn't think of anything to say. He guessed he was in learning mode.

"Anyway, we'll try to do it my way. And, by the way, I

haven't ever tried anything like this before. But I know going in shooting would not work. So what about your buddy?"

"I'll call him right now." Bailey pulled out his phone, plugged into the cigarette lighter, and dialed Lance's shop.

The phone rang only three times, "Yo, Bailey, what's up?"

"Hold on, Lance, there's somebody here I want to hear you, and maybe talk with you. I'll put you on speaker." He did, then, "Lance, meet Heather."

"Hey, Heather."

Heather smiled, "Nice to meet you, Lance, and, you have quite an enthusiastic buddy here."

"Nice to meet you too, Heather, and I agree, Bailey is nothing if not enthusiastic. So, Bailey, talk."

"Well, thanks to Heather I've already found Emma, but, she's kind of in a tight spot, my friend, and we're going to need help getting her out."

"So you want me to come down there?"

"Yes. How soon?"

"Give me three days. You got an address?"

Bailey glanced at Heather. She spoke her address.

"OK, man. See you in two or three days."

"Thanks, Lance."

Then Heather's phone rang. She answered, "Yes…?" then listened for about two minutes, "I understand." She then put her phone back in her purse, started her car, and moved into traffic before she spoke, "This sometimes happens, Bailey. I have to call in sick to the airport, then escort an older gentleman around town tonight, while he drinks and gambols—" She hesitated. Her face definitely didn't smile, "It's what I do…."

Bailey reached for her, and touched her right arm very lightly, then withdrew, "I understand, Heather."

"But don't worry. I'll find out all I can about your little Emma, and I'll make your date with her."

****

That night arrived. Again, Bailey was sleeping very lightly when he heard the garage door opening, then closing, then the house door, then the footsteps, then his bedroom door, and then Heather. The hall light silhouetted her in the doorway. She was so beautiful —*not my type*. She just stood for a moment, then came in and sat on his bed as before, "I made your date, Bailey. Tomorrow night, at seven-thirty, you'll go to the Binghcon Hotel and ask for Trudy. The desk clerk will tell you the room number and give you a key."

"Trudy...?"

"That's her hooker name. The name '*Emma*' was too... *down home,* I guess." Heather glanced at him, "Yes, Bailey, she's a hooker. I realize she's only been gone a little over a month but that's what she is now. A hooker. I keep using these words with you because I know you don't like it. You want to believe that your little Emma is just like she was the last time you saw her, but she isn't, Bailey. She might never again be as you want her to be. You have to get this accepted, so that when you do see her, you'll be able to help her get past how she has been, and how she is." The last Heather said with finality, and released a sigh, and lowered her head, slightly, "She might even *like* what she's doing —some do, for awhile, anyway—and if that's the case...if she *likes* what she's doing, she might even turn you in."

Bailey shook his head. *Emma does not like what she's doing.* No way.

"And there's the possibility she doesn't remember you, Bailey...if she was only seven—"

"She'll remember...!" Bailey's fists flexed open, stiffly. He knew Heather was right, and only trying to prepare him, "I'm sorry, Heather. I know you're just trying to help."

"Yes. I am, and the worst is yet to come. If she *likes* what she's doing, she's not going to want to leave, and if she also doesn't remember you...."

Bailey touched her arm, right above her hand, and squeezed gently, and shook his head, "I know, Heather, and I'm doing my damnedest to get my head wrapped around everything, but I keep believing everything will work out OK. I have to believe that."

After a few seconds Heather put her hand over Bailey's and squeezed back, then patted, then withdrew, "I'm going to bed now, my new friend." She smiled at him, "Then I'm going to sleep at least till noon tomorrow. Again, you just help yourself to breakfast." She stood, turned toward the door but then turned back and again kissed his cheek, as before just a quick peck.

Bailey watched her slip through the door. *Not my type, huh.* He no longer was certain she really meant that, but, again, for anything to change between them Heather would have to cause the changes.

****

Emma had been doing everything she was told for a month. She was done with that. More than done. The next time she had a chance she would run. She made sure that she was last to climb into the van and got the seat on the left side closest to the back door. Then the man crawled in, closed the door, and did not lock it. Sometimes he didn't. He maybe forgot, maybe just got lazy, or maybe was getting too trusting.

Emma didn't care the reason. The man, the *older* man, still on his knees, looked around. There were no open seats. Maybe he would go up in front. He didn't, and when the van began to move he just sat down where he was. Emma glanced at the door handle. It faced up. All she had to do was push it and both doors would pop open. The man was close but not blocking it. When they stopped she would push him in the throat and scream her professional tennis scream and she would get past him and out the door, and run.

Twenty minutes passed. Usually it took thirty, but the van began slowing down. She looked forward but couldn't really see anything, but then she never could. The partition didn't shut them off completely but they also couldn't see out very well. She felt the van hitting bumps. That seemed unusual too, as always before the street had been very smooth. She didn't care. This was the moment she had been waiting for. She would escape, she'd go to the police and she'd come back and rescue her friend Alexis.

The van stopped. In that heartbeat Emma was off her seat, screamed her professional tennis scream and hit the man in throat at the same time, then hit the door handle and was out the door. But in the country yet! At that realization she hesitated just a fraction of a second, then grabbed her high-heeled shoes off and began to run, but didn't get far. The man from the passenger-side seat was young like her, and caught her, and hit her in the back of her head with a closed fist.

Emma saw stars and fell, all the way to her front, and got sand in her mouth.

"Little bitch!"

She barely saw the man but did see him again raising his fist. She didn't care. Let them beat her. Let them kill her. She was done doing whatever they wanted!

The fist didn't arrive. She saw the older man arrive, who must have stopped him. Then they rolled her over and picked her up, the younger one holding her legs, the older man with his arm around her shoulders, "You shouldn't have done that, sweetie," the older man said.

They reached the van, opened the door, and tossed her in. Emma crawled up to where Alexis sat and looked up at her. Alexis then broke all rules and took Emma into her arms and hugged her, but didn't speak. The older man crawled in and locked the back door, and took the seat Emma had earlier sat on.

"Take us in!" the older man shouted, "I don't know why the hell you stopped!"

"Christ! I had to take a leak!" the driver shouted back, "You should have had the door locked!"

"Fine! It's locked now. Take us in. Alexis with take Trudy's spot tonight and Alexis' date will just have to go without."

Evidently the older man was in charge. Emma guessed it didn't matter. She had tried to escape and failed.

Fifteen more minutes passed. They reached the hotel. The other girls were escorted in while the older man stayed. Emma moved to behind the passenger seat and cowered in the corner, as far as she could get. Her stockings were torn, her dress was torn, and the heel on one of her shoes was broken. What would they do to her? She wondered, but right then was having trouble caring.

The older man stayed in the back with her and never let his eyes leave her. He had always seemed a bit friendly before. She had even spoken with him a couple times, but now he seemed as cold as all the rest. Maybe colder, as he maybe *had* come to trust her, maybe even *like* her, but now she could see he hated her. She didn't care. She just pulled herself a little tighter into her corner and closed her eyes.

"You're a pretty girl, Trudy," he said coldly, "You could have made a lot of money with us."

"Yeah!" Emma cried, "Degrading myself every night! And my name's *not* Trudy!"

The man just laughed.

****

Exactly at seven-thirty Bailey entered the Binghcon Hotel. There were several people in the lobby, men and women both, and none looked like they were there for the same reason as him. The desk clerk didn't smile, was as if he knew what Bailey was there for, so might as well remove all doubt, "Trudy, please."

The clerk took about two seconds to respond, "Room 419," and handed over the key.

Strange, that was all Heather said to say. One would have thought there would have been some attempt at hiding what was happening. The key felt foreign in his hand. He *so* didn't belong there, but then, Emma didn't belong there either. He gripped the key and walked to the elevator. The door opened immediately and a man stepped in with him, "Do you have the money?" he asked, as soon as the door closed.

Now he really was surprised, but again, he didn't know what he had expected, and didn't really expect somebody would collect the money right there in the elevator. Didn't prostitutes on television do their own collecting? They probably didn't trust Emma that much yet—yes, that was it! They wouldn't trust Emma because she would be so against them, and against what she was doing. He *believed* that, and he *believed* Emma had not forgotten him and that she would leave this life willingly, gladly. "Yes." He reached in his coat breast pocket and grasped the envelope and pulled it out and handed it over and could barely believe he was handing three thousand dollars to a complete stranger. Lucky Lance had offered him more money than he asked for.

The man took the envelope, opened it, fanned the money once, closed it again and stuck it into his own pocket. On cue the elevator door opened. The man stepped off and two other patrons entered, a man and woman, both tastefully dressed. What a place for a brothel. It passed perfectly for an abode of the well-to-do. The elevator door started to close. Bailey had enough time to ensure himself he was on the fourth floor, then quickly stepped off. On the wall in front of him were two signs. The one to the left pointed to numbers 415 and smaller, the one to the right pointed to numbers 416 and larger.

His heart gave a thunderous beat. He was getting so close; his breathing began coming in short, quick breaths like he couldn't get enough air to even breathe. He turned to his right and walked quickly, and wondered, what would he say to her? What if she doesn't remember him at all? She probably won't. But surely she'll remember his name. How many hundred thousand times had he heard Emma say, *"Bailey, can I do this?" "Bailey, can I do that?"* And she always said his name.

He walked faster, looking left, 416, looking right, 417, looking left, 418—*this is it!*

He looked right—what the hell! No 419! What? He heart nearly beat right out of his chest, then he finally looked at the other side...419. Whoever put the numbers on the doors had really screwed up. He looked at the other wall again. The numbers continued on the wrong wall. He took a really deep breath. His body shook as a long breath left him. For a second or two he just totally relaxed and shook his head. Then the short breaths started again. He tightened his fists, then relaxed them again. Emma was right beyond that door. What would be so hard just to take her out of there, go down the fire escape and get the hell out of there right now? He *really* considered it, but it probably was a pretty stupid thing to do. Heather knew this business. He didn't.

He raised his hand to knock—wait! No. He had a key. There was a reason for their madness. She was probably all ready in bed, waiting for him, then he realized the key was still pressed in his fist. He opened his hand and looked. Sure enough. It had even left an impression. He put it in the keyhole, and turned it. The lock snapped, not loudly. Right, a loud snap would ruin the mood. He felt a short breath leave him, and again, then he took another deep one through his nose, held it, and let it out through his mouth, slowly, then pushed the door open, stepped in, and again locked it.

A soft light from the Las Vegas streets filled the room. White or beige walls with walnut trim. A lush burgundy carpet. Elegant straight-backed chairs on either side of a fine dresser. Other lavishly-stuffed chairs sat in the corners. To his left a nearly-dark bathroom but shining clean. For a few seconds he wondered about the lavish room. Maybe Emma *did* like living like this. Maybe—*probably*—better than the life she had at home, for sure better if her so-called guardians would allow her to get abducted and sold! For a few seconds he just fumed, more at himself for abandoning Emma when she was yet a child, then at Auntie Evelyn. He walked a ways further till he could see the bed, and could see a woman lying in it with her bare back turned. His side of the bed was turned down, waiting for him.

He stared at that bare back. *She's a fully-grown woman now.* But all he could think of was a tiny child, what he remembered, a child who had depended on him to love her and hug her and protect her, and he had let her down, he had abandoned her.

He walked to the bed, then continued just standing there, wondering what Emma would be thinking, because she would be expecting a man she didn't know. But of course she didn't know him either. He swallowed, and let out a breath, then sat down in the turned-down spot, "Emma…?"

"What…?" She didn't sound right. She sounded surprised, like he would have expected her to, but she didn't sound quite as he thought she would have sounded. She turned to him very slowly and pulled the covers to her throat, "I'm not Emma."

Bailey had no idea what to say; he didn't have enough breath to barely say anything, "What? Why? Where is she?"

The young girl's eyes were huge, "I don't know. They maybe took her away…."

Dear God. "Why?"

"She tried to escape tonight. They took her back to punish her. Sometimes…they don't come back at all. Have…you had Emma before?"

"She's my daughter." Easier to tell her that then to jump right into a long explanation. Anyway, Emma *should* have been his daughter.

The girl brought her hand to her mouth, "I'm sorry…I wish…," then didn't finish.

"What do you wish?"

"I wish my daddy would come for me."

"Where's your daddy?"

"I don't know. He abandoned my mom and me when I was too small to remember him."

"What about your mom? Where is she?"

"She…kicked me out. A year ago."

"I'm sorry." He touched her shoulder through the bed

cloth, "What's your name, sweetheart?"

"Alexis."

"May I call you Alex?"

"Yes."

"Well, Alex, if at all possible, when—*if*—I find Emma, when it comes time to leave, I'll try to get you out of here too."

"Thank you." The girl relaxed but kept the covers pulled up to her chin, "What do you want to do now?"

"Well, I guess we'll just wait. Nobody will check on us, right?"

"No, but I mean, well, I know you paid a lot of money… and…it's not like I haven't done it before…and, well, I wouldn't mind."

Bailey patted her shoulder and smiled, "I appreciate you saying that, Alex, but tonight you get to rest."

"Thank you." Tears filled her eyes. She choked, then tears began gushing. She had to cover her mouth.

Bailey looked for a tissue, then went in the bathroom and got a handful of toilet paper. When he came back she was in full sob mode. He handed her the tissues, smiled again, then walked to the window. The shade was still up. He pulled it down, then stood to the side and looked out at the street. Many people were about but two men stood in front of a coffee shop and didn't appear to be in any hurry to go anywhere. He suspected some of the other rooms also had his kind of paying customers in them too. He also suspected there were men watching all exits, just in case someone was stupid enough to try to run, as he had been thinking earlier. He guessed he definitely would listen to Heather.

He came back to the bed and sat again. Alexis had her tears under control. "So, Alex, do you know Emma?"

"Yes. She's my closest friend, but it's hard to have friends. If they see somebody getting too friendly they try to turn you against each other, even some of the other girls will tell. It's hard, sir."

"I understand." Yes, but he didn't *really* understand. He understood, yes, what he couldn't do was comprehend how men could treat young girls in this way. Heather was right. Even with his eight years in the army he had evidently led a sheltered life, not quite under a rock but he guessed *close*, "When they bring you here, well, could you find your way back?"

"No, they make us ride in the back of a closed-in van, and they never allow us to go outside when we're at the house. I *can* tell you it's close to the city limits. because it doesn't take long to get here. And, from the house I can see open country in the distance."

"You said Emma tried to escape just tonight. What happened?"

Alexis told him, and went into great detail, "I'm afraid of what might happen to her. Emma has tried to cooperate—well, I should say, she has tried hard to *convince* them she was cooperating, but from the very first she talked about trying to escape."

That's my girl. The thought pleased Bailey, that his Emma was being brave and courageous, but also caused him concern.

They were both quiet for a time, then Alexis spoke, "Sir, if Emma would have been here tonight, would you have tried to take her away?"

"I did think about it, but, mainly I just wanted to be sure it was her, so that I could make plans for what to do next." And he sure didn't know what could happen next, "Well, Alex, now I have to know how this works. What time do the *johns* leave? And then I suppose you just stay here until they come for you, is that right?"

"Yes, and the *johns* leave anytime between six and seven-forty-five A.M."

"And they come for you at eight? All of you?"

"Yes, we're to be dressed and ready exactly at eight, and

we go out the back door."

"Always the back door?"

"Yes."

"OK, Alex, I promise I will try to get you out of here, and, if you see Emma...."

"I'll tell her, sir."

"Good. Now let's both try to get some sleep. If you don't mind I'll lay here beside you but on top of the covers."

"I don't mind, sir." Alexis sent a radiant smile, "Goodnight, sir."

"Goodnight, Alex."

****

Morning came. Bailey awoke at six A.M. He glanced at Alexis. She slept on, but some time in the night she had moved closer to him and had put her hand on his arm. Good. He definitely would try to get her out too. He then moved her hand, pulled the blanket and spread up to fully cover her, then went to one of the straight-backed chairs to put his shoes on, then rose and started for the door."

"Sir...?"

"Alex, I was trying not to wake you."

Keeping the covers up to her neck, Alexis moved to the near side of the bed, then sat up, "I want to hug you, sir, to thank you, for last night."

"No thanks necessary, Alex." He moved to the bed, "But, if you want to I would like your hug." He sat down beside her and opened his arms.

She put her arms around him and hugged him tight, "Thank you. I will never forget this."

He hugged her tightly back, then patted her shoulder, "You are very welcome, and don't you give up." He rose, "I'll be back for you."

"Like the Terminator?" She smiled.

He smiled back, "Not quite like the Terminator," then waved and headed for the door, and hoped he wasn't raising a false hope in the girl. At the door he unlocked, then held onto the knob for a few seconds, knowing there could be trouble in the hallway, but he opened and stepped out. Nobody. He moved quickly to the elevator.

On the main floor again he passed the desk. The same clerk was there. He wondered if the man lived in the hotel, and wondered how much he got paid for his part of the brutal scheme. Plenty, probably, because his silence was necessary. The clerk didn't look up as Bailey passed and dropped the key on the counter, which satisfied Bailey.

Outside he found a quiet street, and started the two blocks to the main drag, where all the action was. In the 24/7 city the main drag would have plenty of taxis. He soon was there and hailed one. The driver reminded him of Will Smith. The man had the same build and bright eyes, the same charisma. Bailey felt he had the right driver, so made his request, "I would like to go two blocks straight ahead, then turn right and go two blocks, slow down at the intersection, then go another block, turn...left, I think, return to the main drag and let me out."

The cab driver gave him a look, "You aren't planning a robbery, are you?"

"No, sir. So, you got it?"

"Yep. Two blocks straight ahead, turn right two blocks, slow down, go around that whole block slowly but not slowly enough to attract attention, then go another block straight ahead, turn left, and right back here. Yeah, I've got it even better then you do, man. You want to scope out the Binghcon Hotel, don't you?"

"You got it, man. Thank you, and one more thing."

"Yeah...?"

"If you get a short and quick fare, fine, but other than that

I want you to park and wait for my call, and then—by the same route we're going to take—I want you to come get me at a place yet to be determined, and be ready to tail somebody without getting caught. How about that?"

"You got it, man." The man who looked like Will Smith turned around, grinned widely, and stuck his hand out, "I'll take a hundred bucks right now, my man, then I'll park and there won't be any fares till I hear from you."

****

Bailey felt somewhat surprised that just two blocks from the main Las Vegas strip there could be shady alleys and dark spaces between buildings, almost as if it were ordered just for him to spy on the Binghcon Hotel. Just a half a block away he could see not only the back door but the one fire escape, so if the girls were brought out as usual he would see them. He hoped they wouldn't come past him because he had no place to hide if they did.

Some time passed. He wished he still smoked, not that smoking would have made the time go by more quickly but it would have *seemed* to. He remembered his smoking days as not being that bad. He never felt exactly out of breath from it and usually only smoked after getting something finished, a sort of pleasurable treat. Rarely did he smoke as a habit, as so many claimed "*...something to do!*" No, but he did sometimes smoke in a situation like this, not that he had ever exactly before been in a situation like *this*.

But just thinking about it must have helped, because a van with no side windows pulled up to the back of the hotel, and two men quickly entered the back door. Another twenty minutes went by. Then the door opened and first a man came out, who first looked in all directions, then four absolutely gorgeous young girls, including Alexis, then the guy who had entered the elevator with him and took his money. The girls were herded into the back of the van and the two guys scrambled into the front. The third man crawled in back and closed the door. Then they started out and turned toward Bailey. He laid down flat and put his suit coated arm in front of his head and hoped he would just look homeless. And of course the people in the van had no reason to even look his way.

In just a few seconds he heard them pass. He leaped up and dialed the cab. About three minutes later the cabbie arrived. He barely could believe his luck and climbed in, "A dirty old green van with no windows."

"I met'em coming over here, man. Don't worry."

Five minutes more after a few tight corners Bailey could see the van ahead, with about three other vehicles between them. The cabbie seemed to know what he was doing, "I'll stay about this far back, man. That way we'll have time to slow down or speed up, or even stop if need be."

"You're doing a great job. Thanks."

"Don't s'pose you want to tell me what's going on though, huh?"

"I guess you deserve to know. I think I have a good lead on finding my daughter." Bailey again felt a little strange telling yet another person that Emma was his daughter. Emma maybe wouldn't even like that, course she need never know that he had ever said such a thing.

"Runaway? Or sex slave?"

"That van we're following has four of the youngest, most beautiful girls riding in the back that I hope to ever see in this lifetime. So I would say sex slaves. I don't know if they all are—I mean, maybe some are there by choice, or even moles planted by the ring, just to keep tabs on the other girls, report any unhappiness…or whatever, I guess.

"Your daughter among'em?"

"No. I'm afraid she got caught trying to escape."

"And…you *know* that?"

"Not for sure. I spent the night with one of the other girls."

"What?" The cabbie sounded—and *looked*—somewhat irritated.

Bailey didn't blame him, "Not to sleep with, man. I paid the money, and thought I was getting my daughter. But I didn't."

"Quite a disappointment, I imagine."

"Yes, but the girl I did get knew my daughter, or at least knew of her, and told me Emma had gotten caught trying to escape."

"Emma…?"

"Yes."

"That's a pretty name, and by the way, our van just took a left."

"OK."

"I'll just slow down, man. We'll look down that street and decide if we dare follow."

They crossed the intersection. It appeared that the road soon would lead into the country. "OK, go another block make two lefts and back onto their street. We'll go as far as we dare, and don't worry. If things get dicey we'll quit following."

"OK, man."

They got back to the street just as the van disappeared. They followed. When the van appeared again…,"OK, turn onto this street coming up," Bailey said, "We don't want them to think they're being followed. I don't know. Maybe they never think they get followed. And maybe they think their girls are not cared about or missed…or loved."

"Except for your Emma."

"Yes, my Emma is cared about and missed and loved, and she's giving them trouble, so we have to get her away from them." And with a car other than a taxi he could go down that road and maybe see the van parked at some house, or see another road leading off, and he needed to get a map so he could see where that road led to, hopefully another town, or at least another highway. In the Nevada desert like this, a stranger, like himself, would never know. Because if he saw the van he would have to keep going and hope he could turn somewhere without going all the way to the next state, "OK, man, take me to a restaurant on the other side of town. I've got some thinking to do."

The cabbie waved.

About ten minutes later they pulled up at an Applebee's. Bailey looked at the register, "Holy shit!—Sorry, man, I'll pay you. I just wasn't expecting—"

"Take it easy, man. You've already given me a hundred, and I've come to like you. So, we're even, and here's my card." He held it up, "If you ever need help in a hurry you call."

Bailey grasped the card, "You are a gentleman."

"And a scholar." The Will Smith-looking cabbie grinned.

"And a scholar, man. You bet." Bailey jumped out and waved as the cabbie drove away.

****

Inside he ordered, then put in a call to Heather. She answered on the third ring, "Hi, Bailey."

"Wow! You've already got my number logged in?"

"I do. I saw it yesterday morning when you called your friend. I notice things, Bailey. Another reason I'm able to stay alive. So, did you get to see your little Emma?"

"No. Another girl came in her place. She knows Emma, though, and said Emma tried to escape."

Heather didn't answer. A very silent moment went by, then, "That's not good news, Bailey."

"I know, and it means we have to get to her, that is, I—*I* have to get to her. I can't ask you to get involved any further, Heather. I don't want you to get hurt, so I'm going to rent a car —"

"No. *I* will decide how involved I want to get, Bailey. My date for tonight is not for all night I have found out. Believe it or not this date for tonight is just for wining and dining, then I'll see to it he gets to his hotel room, say goodnight, and then I'll pick you up and…we'll see what happens."

"You're sure…."

"I'm sure. Now, where are you? I'll come get you and take you home—" *Take me home, yes!* "—go on my date, then I'll come back and get you." He felt kind of guilty after his last thought. Heather had already told him more than once that he wasn't her '*type,*' so a relationship with her shouldn't be in his mind at all, and it wouldn't be, except for what she said, the words, '*take you home*' just sounded so…nice.

"I'm at Applebee's on…" He looked at the menu and rattled off an address, "Can I order you something?"

"Sure. Order me a BLT, and I'll be there in about fifteen minutes."

"OK."

****

Bailey woke, and felt like he hadn't slept at all. The green digitals of the clock read 12:30. He expected Heather home at any moment, so might as well get dressed. She had said it: She would get as involved as she wanted to, so he wanted to be ready to go when she got home. Enough light entered the house from streetlights, and, luckily, it had occurred to him that a light anywhere in the house would tell the driver of a car returning Heather that she had company. He supposed she *did* have occasional company but '*no lights*' was probably a good policy.

They hadn't talked much at Applebee's, just small talk, nothing about the upcoming night and exactly what they would do, but Bailey had filled her in about the night spent with the girl who *wasn't* Emma. Mainly, one sentence stuck with Bailey. Heather's brow had risen—a *lot*—when she asked, "You *slept* with her?" Meaning she, maybe, *did* care. And his answer, "On top of the covers."

Then neither spoke for several minutes. Bailey hoped his answer was the right one, and, obviously, Heather had wanted to know. But for herself? Hoping for herself to maybe have a relationship with Bailey? Or had she just wondered if he was jerk enough to have taken advantage of the situation and had sex with that young girl? He wouldn't blame her if that's what she thought, and was glad she had asked, so that he could clear the air and let her know that 'no' he had not been a jerk. He had been a jerk plenty of times in his life, but not *that* night.

Ten minutes later he waited at the kitchen table and had downed two cookies. He considered that it was a very nice room, a very nice house, and a very nice woman in charge of it.

Then he heard a car door close. He listened for the small garage door to open. It did, and closed. Another moment passed. Then a key in the house door. He *hoped* it was Heather. The door opened and the light came on, and it *was* Heather, "Did you sleep?"

"Yes, but not that well."

"So you're ready to go?"

"Yes." He hunched his shoulders, opened his hands, shook his head, didn't know what else to do.

"All right. Just a moment." Heather went to her bedroom and came back carrying a .45 semiautomatic pistol just like his own, and two clips, "Do you know how to use this?"

"Yes. I even own one, but couldn't really bring it on the flight."

"No, of course not." She handed it over, "Don't load it till we get there."

"Right." Wherever *there* was, and whatever they were headed for.

****

While driving to wherever they were driving, Bailey decided it was time to share some information, "I have a name, Heather."

"Oh...? Who?"

"This guy up in Montana, where I come from, told me.

Fletcher Martin." Bailey could actually hear the long sigh leaving Heather. He wondered what kind of nerve he had struck, "Do you know him?"

She stayed quiet for several more seconds, "I do, Bailey. He's my contact. He's the one who gets me all my...*dates*."

Which meant to Bailey that if the man ever connected her to him she would be finished, but Bailey was pretty sure he was going to ask her to leave with him anyway, but, of course, only after they found and rescued Emma. Without Emma...well, Bailey didn't care to think about that, they *would* get Emma, "Did you know that he goes around *buying* little girls?"

"*Little* girls?"

"I mean young girls, like Emma."

"No. I didn't know he did that. I guess I thought he was— I don't know what I thought—nice, I guess. I didn't want to think about what else he was involved with. Sort of like the wives of big gangsters. They don't know what their husbands do for a living and they don't exactly *want* to know...so, did he buy Emma?"

"Yes, from a guy named Jackson. I don't know how much he paid."

"You can be sure he paid plenty. Those young girls bring in thousands."

"Do you like this...*Fletcher*? I mean—has he *meant* something to you?"

"I guess I thought he did...I guess I even thought...if I ever get out of this business it would be thanks to him."

"And now?"

"And now I just want to stop him, Bailey, and I want to help you help your Emma."

"OK. Good. Will Fletcher be where we're going?"

"Yes, very likely. The girls stay in the house, and the guys stay in like a bunkhouse. There's usually two of'em."

"Do they ever…bother, the girls?"

Heather didn't answer, but she did glance at him. Her face showed…his best guess was pain, so, yes, likely the boys bothered the girls quite often. He didn't like thinking of his little Emma in that kind of situation. But she was.

"I have a woman's name too, Heather…*Fleurette*."

Heather, again, didn't answer right away, but even in the dark he could see that, yes, Heather knew Fleurette, so he waited.

"Fleurette helps during the training sessions, not physically, that I know of. She's there to make sure the girls aren't hurt. That's not quite right. The girls definitely get hurt. Some are even virgins, and Fleurette does the check for virginity. You see, they have a list of clients who are willing to pay…" She shook her head, "Unbelievable amounts of money for virgins, then she goes along with the girl for…the event." She again shook her head, "I don't know, Bailey. The poor girls have spent—up till then—a lifetime of saving themselves and for what? Some old bastard with cold hands and a lot of money. Was your Emma a virgin?"

"I don't know. I'd…like to think she was. Anyway, Jackson, the one who gave me the small amount of information I have—until I found you, well, Emma I guess was cleaning house for him. I guess she usually was able to leave most houses before the owners came home, as she worked for a maid business that paid her. But her aunt's boyfriend also provided cleaning leads. This deal with Jackson was one of Merle's leads, and, I guess this night…I guess she didn't leave in time, and I guess Jackson told it all around all about it."

"And he didn't have to pay for the virginity thing."

"Right. I guess he just takes young girls when and where he can find them. I would like to shut his lights off for good."

Heather began slowing down, "OK, Bailey. Pretty quick we're going to park and walk, and I hope you know that we will really be showing our hand tonight. I mean if Emma isn't here…."

"I understand." Bailey understood all right, but even if Emma wasn't there he couldn't exactly imagine quitting.

Heather turned onto an approach, then drove a little farther and, after making a couple turns and maneuvers, backed in and parked behind what looked like a highway billboard. They sat for a minute, then Heather spoke, "The house is about a half mile farther on the highway, then about a quarter mile north. We'll determine what cars are in the yard, and how many. If just one car…well, we'll hope it's Fletcher's, as he's the only one who will know anything about Emma."

Something finally occurred to Bailey, "Heather, is that who picks you up and brings you home?"

"Yes." She sighed once.

They got out. Both continued being quiet. Bailey was pretty sure she didn't want to talk further about Fletcher Martin. He came around to her side of the car. Where Heather stood the moon brightened her face. He saw her so clearly, and wanted to go to her, but knew it still wasn't time, maybe never would be. They had made a good team so far. No use ruining everything by trying to get personal.

Heather's face was absolutely sober, and she evidently agreed, "Well, let's go—you got the gun?"

"Yes."

"Load it."

Bailey went through the motions of loading, cocking, and releasing the hammer.

"OK. Let's do it."

****

About a half hour later they stopped behind a building. The moon shone into the yard almost like day. No movement anywhere. Both buildings were quiet and dark. The house had a padlock on the outside. Christ, the occupants, probably several young girls, would be in trouble if a fire. Just one car sat close to the bunkhouse door.

"You should go in alone, Bailey. If Emma *isn't* here, if they don't know I'm involved, maybe I'll be able to find out more later."

"OK." Bailey moved to the front door and was surprised to find it not locked. He just turned the knob and entered. Moonlight came in from the one window and lit up the one bed he could see. Definitely a body there. Did he want a light? Yes? No? He decided '*yes.*' If there was more than one man he would need light, so began feeling along the wall by the door for a switch, and found it, and flicked it.

Slowly two dim florescent tubes began fluttering on. He glanced quickly about the room. Three other bunks but only the one body. He felt the gun in his hand, carefully placed his finger alongside the trigger, then approached the bunk, and stopped just outside the man's reach, then reached over with the gun and gently tapped his head with the barrel, then withdrew and gripped the gun with both hands and kept it pointed slightly up, "Fletcher Martin?"

The man opened his eyes—about fifty, black hair, slim— then closed them again, "Who the fuck are you?"

"I'm Emma's father. I came to take her home."

"What...?" The man opened his eyes again and shaded them, "You are about the craziest fuck I've ever seen."

Bailey jerked the gun toward the man's leg under the blanket, "Where *is* she?"

"Whoa!"

Bailey cocked the gun, "Speak then! Where *is* she?"

"She's not here!" The man didn't sound too frightened.

"Look, I haven't shot you yet but I will, if you don't start talking. So where is she?"

"I sold her."

"What? *Why?*"

"Because she wouldn't cooperate! I've never had to deal with such a stubborn little bitch."

Bailey brought the gun back to aim at the man's head. He left it cocked.

"It was either sell her or shoot her! And she was worth way too much money to shoot!"

"You're a real bastard, Martin."

"How the hell do you know my name?"

"Does the name Jackson mean anything to you? He described you too, as the man who does all the buying and selling…so keep talking. Who too? And how long ago?"

Martin sat up and swung his legs out, "Mind if I get dressed?"

The man looked to be about the same size as Bailey. So unless he was a '*Golden Glover*' or a martial arts expert, Bailey figured if it should come to a fight he would have at least half a chance. But Heather was there too, but it had sounded a bit like she might still consider him somewhat of a boyfriend, so he wasn't sure of help. He stepped back and kept the gun leveled, and cocked, "Yes, I mind. Answer my questions, or I will start pulling this trigger, starting with your footies." He lowered the gun and aimed at Martin's right foot, "And believe me, you'd be good and crippled for life."

Martin raised his hand to partially shield his face, "All right! She's still here—not *here*—but her buyer hasn't picked her up yet."

"Oh, man, guys like you…I'd like to kill all of you. So where *is* she?"

"She's close. There's another house, about a mile away… I'd have to show you, so can I get dressed?"

"Just a minute." Bailey stepped back to the door and opened it, "Heather, can you come in?"

Bailey didn't take his eyes off Martin, whose jaw dropped

when he saw Heather, evidently surprised. Heather entered.

"Heather…," Martin said, "What the hell? I thought you and I—"

"There was never a *'you and I,'* Fletcher. I was just surviving. You got me into this…racket, and now I'm finally getting out."

"You bitch…."

So Heather wasn't exactly aligned with Martin, but he would still wait and see, but what she said *'getting out'* had sounded positive, "OK, Martin, get dressed then—wait! I'll check your clothes first. Bailey walked to what looked like Martin's clothes, "These it?"

Martin nodded, and appeared disappointed. Bailey found a small handgun in the jeans-pocket, and, under everything, laid a shoulder holster with a larger gun and two clips, "No wonder you wanted to get dressed." He returned to Heather and handed her gun back to her, then checked Martin's gun, also a 45. It was loaded but not cocked. He pulled the slide back and released the hammer, then handed that one to Heather also, then checked the smaller gun, also a semiautomatic, also loaded. He pulled the slide back on it too, released the hammer, then put it in his right front suit pocket, "OK, Martin, we have all the firepower, so I almost hope you try something stupid. *Now,* you can get dressed."

He glanced at Heather and hoped for, yes, a smile, not a big one but a smile nonetheless, then he took back Martin's gun.

****

Outside, Martin immediately started for his car.

"Hold it, Martin. Heather, would you mind going after your car? We're going to need it."

"OK, Bailey. Give me twenty minutes. When I can see where I'm going I'll jog." She left. Luckily they had the moon for light.

Again Martin looked disappointed. The man must have

thought they would both just jump in with him. The man moved to his car, then leaned against the right front fender, "You seem to be thinking of everything."

"Oh, not everything I don't suppose. After all I've never had to come after my daughter like this before." Again he felt strange referring to Emma as his daughter. He hoped she would understand.

"So what did you do to cause her to run away?" Martin asked, a definite smirk on his face.

"She was abducted and sold and bought by *you*."

"Sure. That's what they all say, but in my experience Daddy's girl usually has a reason for leaving, so, I ask again, *'What did YOU do to little Emma?'*"

Just hearing Fletcher Martin speaking Emma's name made Bailey want to pound the man into the ground, beat him and then kill him...but, for awhile, he needed him, so decided to get some inside information that only a man like Martin could tell him, "What do your girls tell you...that happened to them?"

"To be honest—and I know that's what you're expecting from me—little Emma didn't tell me anything about her daddy. In fact, I don't remember hearing about anything that little Emma told anyone, so whatever it was it must have been bad."

It was bad all right. Bailey had allowed other family members to crowd him out. Instead of fighting for Emma he had allowed it to happen. He had abandoned her at a very young age, no other word for it. He *abandoned* her. But at the time it had seemed like the right thing to do, and the word *'abandonment,'* then, never entered his mind. Auntie Evelyn was married to Merle —who at the time seemed like an all right guy—so Bailey had allowed the crowding out to happen. And then he had completely lost touch.   He never forgot Emma, of course, but also never heard a thing about her, didn't know if she had ever needed him. And he still didn't know, but he did feel he had at least tried to stay in touch by sending birthday cards to the address he was pretty sure was correct. But once she got older he should have tried to get back in touch, but he *didn't* try. He wasn't sure why—not true! He *did* know why. He feared she wouldn't remember, or plain wouldn't want anything to do with him. So, rejection was his big fear. He did not want Emma to reject him, so, he also had not had the balls to give her the *chance* to reject him.

If Emma would have gotten any encouragement from him —besides birthday cards—she maybe would have came to him had she needed help, or even if she had just wanted someone to talk to. So he was hoping to get another chance. He would not abandon her again.

"But, as you can probably imagine," Martin was continuing, "Some of the girls have told some hair-raising stories, and even *I* am surprised at how many daddies have turned to molesting their own daughters—and I'm talking about *blood-daddies*! Sure, step-fathers do it too, but in all the young girls I've known, only one—no wait! Two, I think. Two complained about her step-daddy. Reckon that surprises you some, don't it?"

"I guess I've never had cause to do any research."

"Ha! Right! And never had time to give to your daughter either! Am I right?"

"I've made some mistakes." Strangely enough, Martin was speaking probably the truth, and about Bailey, definitely the truth. After their parting he had given Emma no time at all. He hoped he could make it up to her.

"So, smart guy, you seem to be interested," Martin said, "Did you know that it's estimated up to twenty-five percent of young girls get molested before they're eighteen, and quite often, if not the dad it's a brother, or uncle, or cousin—they figure strangers only account for about ten percent—did you know that?"

"No." Bailey definitely did not know. He was embarrassed and ashamed of the things he didn't know, things that might have helped Emma along the way.

"And another thing," Martin continued, "I've interviewed many of my girls—and by the way, I only buy smokin'-hot eighteen to twenty-five-year-olds. I have a legitimate business here in Nevada and I use only white American girls. My corral has only the very best livestock. I don't bring in girls from foreign countries, and I don't buy kiddies. But there's plenty of scumbags out there who catch'em at much younger ages, twelve, thirteen, even as young as nine, and do you know where they catch'em?"

"If you have a legitimate business why do you have to buy girls, and hold them captive? That door over there has a padlock, on the outside for Christ's sake."

"I buy'em because the smokin'-hot ones don't usually volunteer."

Bailey just shook his head.

"You poor, dumb, fuck. I don't know how many girls run away every year. Hundreds, thousands, I don't know. But they run away, man, and I'll tell you something else. These poor little girls are pushed into modeling by their mommies—who evidently missed their own chance, and daddies too—so they push their daughters to dress and stand provocatively for the cameras. Do you think the perverts out there don't suck up all those ads, and want to taste those little sweetie pies? Do you think those ads have nothing to do with all the sexual perversion these days? Man, even a straight-laced fucker like you, Bailey, must get turned on by some of those photos—and television and the movies! Pimps and prostitutes are glamorized for Christ's sake! And music videos—well, I won't even *try* to describe the damage those videos are doing to America's little girls."

Bailey knew what Martin was describing. He himself had noticed and thought sometimes, too, that even very young girls appeared to be...overly-glamorized, and, yes, made to appear quite sexy, "Straight-laced guys like me might notice, Martin, subconsciously, but we don't act on those thoughts—"

"Sure you don't, but you also allow it to happen! You turn away! And those modeling little girls, they keep getting pushed to be pretty and sexy. It's one beauty contest after another, and there's plenty of goddamn failures. So to create one supermodel how many girls have to lose? I can't tell you for sure, but I will bet that most girls in the sex trade—exotic dancing, pornography, all of it—got her start by failing at modeling and beauty contests, oh, and of course early molestation. In fact, maybe I should add that question to my interview list: '*Did you get your start through beauty contests?*'." Then he laughed.

Bailey was finding it hard to believe that such as man as Fletcher Martin was so well-informed. He absolutely sounded like he had a masters degree in psychology, like a professional on the right side of the law. He almost sounded like he cared about his girls. Maybe in some twisted way he did.

"You probably don't believe a man such as me could have all this knowledge, do you? And you're right. A normal man like me wouldn't. But I did social work for three years, man, I saw the worst of the worst. Homes, I mean. Kids are getting abused and/or molested at home—even *nice* homes—at foster homes, single-parent homes, and do you know the biggest goddamned reason these girls—well, they usually don't come right out and say it, but the homes these girls come from are usually lacking in good, old-fashioned love, true and dependable love from their parents, or whoever their caregivers might be."

"You actually worked with these kids, and now you're doing *this*?"

"Yeah, man, I saw the potential, so I changed careers. And now I repeat, Mister Forbes, what did you do to your little Emma to make her as vulnerable and unloved as she is? Did you come to her in the dark of night? Or, maybe to gain your love, she came to you—"

Bailey could take no more from this man, this monster who made his living from buying and selling young girls like Emma. He laid his gun on the fender of Martin's car, and walked fast, stomping, toward Martin, "God, you're a bastard!"

Even Martin was surprised by Bailey's silly and clumsy advance, and got knocked off his feet, but at the same time he nailed Bailey in the forehead. Bailey had forgotten how unknowledgeable he was about the ways of the real world. It never even occurred to him that a man like Fletcher Martin could even throw such a devastating punch. Those were his exact thoughts as he saw stars and reeled backward, even with his forward momentum he still went down, hard. Martin, too, had lost his balance but regained it very quickly and got past Bailey, and got the gun as Bailey hit the ground, and aimed it at Bailey's head. As Bailey tried to rise after seeing stars he saw Heather in her car approaching, and realized Martin must think Heather really was still on his side, or he surely would have shot at her.

But Heather stopped, stepped out of her car carrying her gun, too, "Don't do it, Fletcher! I swear, I *will* shoot you!"

Martin lay the gun back on the fender then slowly headed for the driver's side of his own car.

"Hold it, Martin," Bailey said, getting up again, maybe somewhat getting a grasp on the real world again, "What do you think you're doing?"

Martin pointed, "Heather's here so we can get going, so you can get to your darling little Emma."

"Fine. But you stay where you are. I'll check your car before you get in. Do you think I'm an idiot?"

Martin threw both his hands up in apparent disgust, "Yeah, I guess I do, after your little attack here I thought just maybe this guy's an idiot...." Martin then returned to the rear fender and leaned against it.

"Heather, I need to check Martin's car for weapons. Will you keep him covered? I mean, if I was a professional I could probably do both, but I'm not"

"And we sure know you're not!" Martin added, then laughed.

"Sure." She smiled, a bigger one than earlier

Course Martin was in the wrong position to see Heather's smile. Bailey continued to feel Heather was surely on his side.

She closed her car door quietly and kept her gun leveled at Martin, "Don't move, Fletcher, because I guarantee I *will* shoot you."

"No you won't, baby. " At that instant, maybe the moonlight hit him just right, but the man was handsome, '*tall, dark, and handsome*' as the old saying went. Bailey didn't blame Heather for being involved with him. True, she probably *didn't* have a choice in the beginning, but now she did.

"We've had too many good times together," Martin was saying, "But, just in case, baby, I won't move."

Bailey, tried to block his mind from the momentary warmth he had just seen pass between them, what he *thought* was warmth, anyway—*not my type*. To empty his mind he fell back on Heather's earlier statements. He had to trust her, so moved quickly to the driver's side of Martin's car, opened the door and immediately saw another .45 in a holster on the front of the seat, right where the driver could easily get it. Martin definitely would have gotten the drop on inexperienced Bailey, and that would have been the end of Bailey's rescue attempt of Emma, "Damn you, Martin! How many guns do you have anyway?"

Martin laughed, "You've found'em all, my friend."

Bailey slipped into the seat, lowered both sun shades and looked in the cubby hole and the storage between the seats. No more weapons, he hoped. He stepped out again, "I'm not your friend, Martin. Do you have permits for all these concealed weapons?"

Again Martin laughed, "I do, and, no, I'm not showing you."

Bailey returned a contrived grin, then glanced at Heather. She wasn't smiling.

"OK," Bailey said, feeling not exactly calm, and wishing Lance could have joined them. In fact, it had been two days. Lance might be at Heather's house, wondering where they were. He had his cell phone off, so wouldn't know if Lance had called.

"Heather, I didn't think of it till right now. Could you dial Lance, and see…?"

"Good idea." She dialed.

"Oh, man, you have his number in your phone too?"

"I told you, Bailey. I'm resourceful."

"Yes, you are."

After a few seconds she spoke into her phone, "Lance, I'm putting you on speaker. Where are you?"

"I'm about an hour from Vegas."

"Bailey leaned close, "We're in kind of a tight spot, Lance. Heather, can you give him directions?"

"Yes."

Bailey listened as the two spoke. It looked like about two hours before Lance could find them. At the end, Bailey again leaned close, "My friend, be careful. These are not nice people we're dealing with."

"Gotcha, my friend. I *will* be careful."

They hung up.

"But we can't wait. Heather, you follow us, and drive with your lights off, if you can, and Martin, I'll ride in the front seat with you, and I swear, by Christ, if you try anything I will shoot your ass!"

****

Fifteen minutes passed. They approached a house that looked about as rundown as photos from the 1930's, "Stop here, Martin," Bailey said, "Get out and stand by the front fender, right now!"

For the third time Martin looked disappointed. He must have still had more weapons hidden in this car, or somewhere, but did get out and stand by the fender.

Bailey moved to Heather, "Turn around and face your car toward where we just came. We might need to leave in a hurry, and I'm sure there's at least one man in there."

"I'm sure there is too, Bailey, so wait for me. I'll go in

too."

"Right."

Quietly, Heather moved the car so that it was facing away, then she joined Bailey, "OK, Martin, you lead the way, turn the light on and then get out of the way."

Martin looked at them and shook his head, positively, then walked to the door.

"Why are you sending him in first?" Heather asked.

Bailey felt dumbfounded, "I don't know…."

Martin stopped at the door, turned, opened his hands and arms, "*Well…?*"

Heather opened her hands and arms too, and shook her head, "I don't know either. Well, you're there, Fletcher. Go ahead."

Martin opened the door, stepped in, turned on the light, then stepped to the side. Bailey was in immediately after him and was shocked by what he saw, and lost his focus, giving Martin enough time to come back with a smashing blow to the side of Bailey's head. Bailey saw stars for the second time and fell, and dropped the gun.

Martin snatched the gun up, cocked it, aimed it at Bailey —and a shot rang out. Bailey heard it. Martin didn't. Dizzy and regaining his wits, Bailey first rose to his knees, then saw Martin fall, blood spurting from his head. The gun fell close to Bailey so he grabbed it, and then saw Heather with her gun leveled at the bed in the corner of the room, where a man, eyes wide, was in bed,

The man in bed was beyond what had taken Bailey's focus, so now he looked again at what had taken his focus, then glanced once more at the man laying on the floor. Plenty of blood still flowing. So no doubt that Fletcher Martin would no longer present a problem.

"Go to her, Bailey, I'll take care of the other guy."

Bailey looked around for a blanket, saw none, so walked to the bed where they guy with the wide eyes was and took his, then walked to the other bed where his darling little Emma lay, naked, uncovered, certainly cold, with all four extremities tied to the bed posts. *The bastards, the sons-of-bitches!* He shook the blanket out and covered her, then went to work untying her, "My god, Emma, I'm sorry, sweetheart. I'm so sorry."

He untied her hands first, then worked on her feet, and saw through peripheral vision that she was rubbing her wrists and staring at him. When he finished with her ankles he snuggled the blanket up to her legs and her sides, then grasped her upper arms, "Emma, are your clothes here?"

"Bai…ley…?" Her voice cracked.

"Yes, Emma." He shook his head and looked into her eyes, those deep blue eyes just like her mother had, "I'm so sorry this happened to you, sweetheart."

She shook her arms away from the blanket and reached for Bailey. He sat down on the bed, lifted the blanket to keep her covered and hugged her back, and listened to her cry, and cry, and she hugged him tighter with every sob.

Finally Heather approached and touched Bailey's shoulder, "The sky's starting to get light, Bailey. I think we need to get out of here."

"You're right. Emma, this is Heather. If not for her help I could never have found you."

Emma looked at Heather, but no smile came to her face.

Heather didn't wait. She found some clothes and put them on the bed.

"Are those yours, Emma?" Bailey asked.

"Yes." Emma continued to look at Heather, but said nothing further.

"OK, I'll hold the blanket up and you get dressed behind it." Bailey stood and held up the blanket, just as he said.

Emma gave him a bright smile and grabbed the clothes, and tried keeping her eyes in Bailey's as she dressed.

"Heather, will you find out if there's a phone here?"

Heather first looked all around, then approached the guy with the wide eyes, "Is there a phone here?"

"No."

"How about a cell phone?" When he didn't answer immediately, Heather pressed on, "Where is it?" When he again didn't answer, Heather cocked the gun and aimed at his head.

"Jesus! In my jacket pocket!" he pointed, in a direction Heather would have to turn her back to get to.

But she didn't turn her back, "How about a gun? You got a gun there under your pillow?" She didn't wait for an answer, just grabbed the pillow, and, sure enough, a gun.

Emma had finished dressing. Bailey hadn't noticed, and was surprised when she covered the distance to the man's gun in about three seconds, picked it up, cocked it and pointed it at the man's head. Bailey moved and got to her just in time to raise her hand as she fired. "Emma, honey, we can't do that."

"He raped me! While I was tied on the bed he just kept on raping me, whenever he wanted!" And many more tears came. Bailey took the gun, uncocked it, and took Emma into his arms again and held her again while she cried and cried and held him tighter with each sob.

Bailey handed the second gun to Heather, who then went to the jacket and found the cell phone, "Bailey, we better go!"

"Yes." Bailey pulled slightly away from Emma but kept one arm around her as he spoke, "Why was she tied up like that?"

"Fletcher's orders!"

"Why?"

"When the buyer comes this morning he'd be able to inspect her."

"You *bastards*!"

"And it made it easier for him to rape me!" Emma cried.

Bailey aimed his own gun toward the man, and cocked it.

"Fletcher gave me permission!" The man's eyes had remained wide the whole time, now they also showed fear, "Fletcher did it too!"

Every word that came out of the man's mouth made Bailey want to shoot him more. But, he had stopped Emma so he couldn't either, "The buyer is coming this morning?"

"Yes! Soon! Maybe eight or nine!"

"Bailey, come on!"

"Coming!" He glanced at Heather then looked one more time at the man, and aimed the gun again, "If I ever see you again…." No point in finishing the threat. He tightened his arm around Emma's waist and started them out.

At the car he asked Emma, "Do you want to sit in front with Heather?"

"No, I—I, want to sit with you, Bailey."

"It's OK, Bailey. You stay with Emma. She wants to be close to you for awhile."

"Yes," Emma said, then finally threw a smile Heather's way.

"All right. You get in. I want to disable these two cars." He wasn't exactly sure how to disable the newer cars, so just took the keys. That would slow them down a bit, anyway. When he returned he crawled into the back seat, closed the door, and smiled at his little Emma.

She smiled back and came to him, and lifted his left arm and put it over her shoulders, then snuggled against him, "I knew you would come for me, Bailey."

She leaned away and showed her tear-streaked face. He saw her really good for the first time. She had rich auburn hair and bright, shining eyes, and freckles, and a smile that could charm the world. She looked just as he remembered her, "Emma, I'm just glad you remember me. How could you possibly *know* I would come for you?"

"Because I've thought about you, Bailey, many, many, times, oh, not every day, but as I've gotten older I've thought of you more, and I've wished you would contact me, and I've thought about contacting you, but I didn't know where you were...well, I knew where you were, I had your return address on the envelopes—but I was *mad* at you! Cause if you didn't try to contact me then I wouldn't you! So, I didn't really try. I guess I was afraid you wouldn't want me again."

"That's how I felt too, sweetheart. I was afraid you would...reject me, I guess"

"But now we both know how wrong we were." Emma gave him a huge smile, "But somehow, when this happened, somehow I just knew that when you found out, you would come for me, and you did." And she snuggled against him again, and Bailey held her, and felt her relax, and soon realized she was asleep.

Until a harder bump woke her, "Bailey!"

"I'm right here, Emma, you're OK. You're safe."

And again she hugged him tightly, and a few more tears came.

And Bailey remembered someone else who had helped in Emma's rescue, "Emma, do you know Alexis?"

"Yes!" She pulled away, "Yes, she's my best friend! Is she OK?"

"Well, yes, I suppose she is. But, well, she's the one who told me that you had tried to escape, and that they took you away, and she didn't know where."

"How did you meet Alexis?"

"That's something I'll tell you about another time, Emma.

Right now I think we should try to get to her too, and we're getting close to the first house again.

****

Another car and probably another man with a gun was waiting for them. The padlock was off the house and likely now locked from the inside, which meant they had to knock. They tried the door first. Yes, locked. Luckily there was no window in the door and no peephole, so the man had to open the door before he could see who. Bailey knocked. After a moment the door opened and the man faced Bailey's gun. Bailey took advantage of the surprised look on the man's face, reached up and grabbed him by the shirt and jerked him outside and to the ground. This man was older and smaller, and, Bailey hoped, less willing to put up a fight, but still kept his gun leveled at his face, but not cocked, "We're looking for Alexis."

"She's not here!"

"Where *is* she?"

"She went to the Binghcon Hotel last night. She should be back any minute!"

Bailey jerked to Heather, "Heather, park your car right where Martin's was last night, and you, mister, head for the bunkhouse." Bailey grabbed his arm and pushed him in that direction. Before they got to the door Heather joined them, "OK, girls, we are going to tie and gag this guy, Emma, you go—wait a minute—any other guys in that house with the girls?"

"No!" The guy answered quickly.

Bailey put the gun against his cheek, "There hadn't better be! OK, Emma, you go to the house and find out who's there and what's going on, but be careful. No matter what this guy said there could be somebody else in there."

"OK, Dad." Emma's face registered surprise. Her hand flew to her mouth, "I'm sorry."

Bailey touched her shoulder, "That's OK, Emma. You go now, OK?"

"Yes." And she hurried away.

"I bet that was music to your ears," came Heather's comment.

Bailey glanced at her and smiled, "Yes, it was."

In a closet in the bunkhouse they found all the rope they needed and soon had the man tied and gagged. "Now you just sit here and be quiet, my man, OK?"

The man shook his head positively.

"OK, let's get back to the main house."

****

Bailey wasn't expecting Emma's quiet comment, "I don't trust Eugenia."

"Who...?" Bailey asked.

"Eugenia. I was hoping she wouldn't even be here. I think she's part of them too."

"Too? Who else do you think is part of them?"

Emma looked at Heather.

"OK, First things first. Let's find Eugenia, Emma."

The found Eugenia, just as she was putting a cell phone into her purse.

Emma went to her immediately, "Who did you just call, Eugenia?"

"Nobody!"

"You're lying!" Emma pushed her. Eugenia fell onto the bed. Emma went right after her and hit her on her head once before Bailey stopped her, "Come on, Emma. If she called the bad guys we have to get out of here."

"What about Alexis?"

Heather gave the answer, "Too late. They're already turning in."

"Why are you pretending to help us?" Emma said, "I know you're with them."

Bailey answered her, "Emma, I know things are a little hard to understand right now, but Heather is on our side. Please believe me."

"All right." Emma moved to Bailey's side.

"You're such a little troublemaker, Emma," Eugenia said, "Things were fine here before you came."

Again Emma turned on her, and Bailey didn't have a chance to stop the sock that followed, that spun Eugenia around and deposited her on the bed again. But just the one. Bailey again held onto Emma, "OK, kid. We have to worry about getting out of here."

Heather was at the window, "They're coming Bailey. Two of them."

"Do they have guns?"

"Yes, and they're drawn."

Bailey had hoped things wouldn't have come to this. He didn't know how he could justify just shooting those men, although, because of the pain they had caused Emma, and probably Heather, and he didn't know how many other women and young girls, he definitely *wanted* to shoot them. And while he was hemming and hawing about it the first man burst through the door and aimed his gun. But Heather was ready, and fired, and dropped her second man with a spurting head wound. Two guys that the legal system would now *not* have to waste any time on.

The second man stopped at the threshold, laid down his gun and raised his hands. Bailey stepped out, grasped his arm and jerked him inside. "Find some rope and tie this guy up." He looked around him. Three more girls had gotten up and were standing around. "Please, girls. We have to move. More might be coming."

The three girls, plus Emma, went to work.

Bailey went out to the van and found three more girls cowering in hiding. They likely had been told not to move, and they definitely had heard the gun shot. Alexis was among them. She recognized Bailey immediately, "Bailey! Don't worry, girls! He's the good guy!"

"Stay on board, girls, we'll be taking this van to the police."

But Alexis jumped down, and threw her arms around Bailey, "You did it, Bailey! Did you find Emma?"

Bailey returned the hug, "Yes, and she's safe."

Heather, Emma, and the other girls all came out right then.

Emma hugged Alexis, then pointed, "Somebody's coming!"

Bailey jerked in that direction. Of course he couldn't know, but maybe just the way the vehicle was moving, very slowly, carefully, like they were checking out a business for a possible future robbery, made the vehicle look ominous. It turned in the driveway, continuing slowly. At least three in the car. "Heather! Do you have your gun handy?"

"Yes."

"Girls, get down behind the van." He felt Emma put her arm around his waist. "Honey, move around behind me," he guided her, "Go the van and tell those girls to get down and hide wherever they can, then you get down behind the van too."

"OK, Daddy. I'm sorry."

Bailey took one second to glance at her. It was as if she was feeling guilty for calling him '*Daddy.*' He definitely would have to talk to her about that, and soon.

The car suddenly speeded up and the back window came open. Out came what looked like the Israeli Uzi—*Tat! Tat! Tat! Tat! Tat! Tat!!!!!*

The bastards didn't seem to care what they shot. It looked like they thought if they couldn't have the girls, then just kill them.

But even before the Uzi began firing they heard sirens in the distance.

All the girls had gotten behind the van and both he and Heather had gotten their guns out and aimed, and both had been able to fire just a second or two after the Uzi began. Blood spurted from the head of the guy in the backseat. That Heather must be an excellent shot. Bailey had aimed his two firings at the windshield. Then the car had speeded away, made a U-turn and came back firing again, making Bailey too dive for the van.

Only when he got safe himself did he see Heather again, lying face down and not moving. Pain and anger made him again stand and hold his gun solidly as the car presented its broad side, and fired his complete clip into the car, which again stopped the guy in the passenger seat. Then the car backed up to behind the van, giving Bailey time to reload.

Then, seemingly from nowhere came another car from the road. It stopped dead in front of the buyer's car. The driver leaped out and professionally fired into the windshield of the buyer's car, which stopped them.

God almighty. How many people had died that morning? Bailey cared about only one, and flew to Heather's side, and rolled her over, and gathered her into his arms, "Heather...," Her entire front was soaked in her blood. Bailey drew her as close to himself as he could and held her tightly—*not my type.*

The thought went through him for the umpteenth time. Maybe he truly wasn't her type but he still would love her and hold her, all night and every night, if she would let him, "Lance! Emma! Somebody! Call 911! Make sure they send ambulances too!"

Heather moved. Bailey threw off his coat and gathered it under her neck, then found two places where she was bleeding and attempted to at least slow it down, "Heather, can you hear me?"

She managed to touch him, "Yes, Bailey."

Two police cars then arrived, about a minute behind them an ambulance. But they needed two or three ambulances, but they would make sure Heather left in the first one, "Emma, go to that ambulance and make sure they come here first."

Emma waved and ran to meet the ambulance.

"Help is coming, Heather. Hang on." He should tell her right now, "Heather, I'm going to keep Emma with me now, and I would love it if you would come too."

She hadn't yet opened her eyes, but now did, "Bailey...." She didn't answer further but he could see in her eyes that she at least would probably not say '*no*'.

The ambulance people arrived and soon had Heather on a stretcher and headed for the vehicle. Bailey rose with them and held her hand. At the door he kissed her cheek. Heather held onto his hand until she couldn't. The door was closed and the ambulance left. Then he felt a hand on his shoulder, both his shoulders, and a voice, a voice that he had for so many years longed to hear again, "C'mon, Dad." He had never expected to ever see Emma again, let alone hear her call him '*Dad.*'

He then turned into the arms of his darling foster daughter, "Emma, sweetheart, I love you, and I've missed you so much for so many years. I thought I would never see you again."

"That's what I thought too, and Alexis told me what you said to Heather, about keeping me with you now."

"Yes, Emma, you're eighteen now. You can live where you want, and do what you want. And if you want to live with me for awhile you can. "

"She said you asked Heather to join us too."

"Yes, I did. Would you like that?

"Yes."

"And what about Alexis?"

"Really? You would take her in too."

"It might get kind of tough living with three beautiful

women, but I would try."

Emma threw her arms around him, "Oh, I love you, Daddy! Do you mind if I call you that?"

Bailey returned the hug completely, "Emma, I love hearing you call me that."

Emma's attention then shifted, "Who's that other guy who helped us?" she asked.

Bailey jerked around, "Lance…." Sure. Of course. Bailey slipped his arm around Emma's waist, and motioned too for Alexis, who then smiled and joined them. Right then he couldn't imagine ever letting Emma go again. He knew he would, of course, but for right then he just couldn't, and she didn't seem to mind and held him right back. Both girls did.

Together and arm in arm they walked to where Lance had kept his gun leveled at the two remaining men in the car until the police, guns drawn, secured the scene.

"Boy!" Lance exclaimed, "You guys have certainly made a mess here.

"You made a pretty good mess, too, my friend," Bailey returned, "Lance, meet my wonderful little girl, Emma, and her good friend Alexis. Emma and Alexis, meet my employer and good friend, Lance. He came all the way from home to help us."

"Montana?"

"Yes, where we will be heading as soon as we can."

Lance smiled and waved, "Hi, Emma and Alexis, and, by the way I called 911 as soon as I got outside the city limits on the way here."

"Good job, my friend. Reckon we'll all have to give statements, and have our guns held up for awhile, or, my gun, I guess. You only brought *my* gun, right?"

"Right."

"And there is more involved here than just here— Eugenia…!"

Emma kept her arm around his waist, and gave him a quick hug, "I hope Eugenia won't have to go to jail."

Bailey glanced at her, remembering Emma punching Eugenia.

"I know," she said, "I was mad at her, and I still am, but I imagine she got caught in this business the same as the rest of us."

"That's my girl, to think that way. You have a good heart, Emma, and there's two other houses, right? And those girls aren't there by choice, either, right?"

"No, they're not, I'm sure," Emma said, "But Eugenia probably knows more than me."

Still another car turned into the driveway. A woman driver and a man passenger, both with huge surprised looks on their faces. Bailey recognized them both. Emma stiffened and pulled away before Bailey could stop her. The car stopped. Emma threw the driver-side door open and dragged the woman out, and began hitting her over and over. Jackson was the passenger. "Cover that guy, will you, Lance?"

Lance moved to the passenger side and Bailey went to the other, and watched Emma throw a few more punches, screaming viciously each time. Fleurette already was on the ground and bleeding. The woman evidently had made Emma really mad somewhere along the way. He would ask Emma to tell him all about it someday. Someday after some time had passed. But for right then he pulled his little girl back into a hug with him.

Emma hugged him right back, "I want my necklace!" she said to the shrinking human trafficker boss lady on the ground, who no longer looked very tough.

"It's in my purse," Fleurette said, and pointed toward the front seat of the car, then started moving toward it.

Emma dropped Bailey and got there first, grabbed the purse, got back to Bailey, opened the purse and withdrew a small handgun. She didn't cock it but did point it at the woman on the ground, then reached in the purse again and withdrew her necklace, "You're lucky it was here, Fleurette...." She made a *'click'* sound and jerked the gun up, as if she had just fired it. Very little doubt that Fleurette received the message.

Bailey had abandoned little seven-year-old Emma eleven years earlier. He knew he would never abandon her again, but he also could see that his little girl had learned many life lessons in her youth, and especially in the past month, and that she had become a young woman and would put those lessons to good use for the rest of her life.

--0--

Printed in Great Britain
by Amazon.co.uk, Ltd.,
Marston Gate.